softspoken

Other Night Shade titles by Lucius Shepard:

Trujillo
Viator

softspoken
LUCIUS SHEPARD

NIGHT SHADE BOOKS
SAN FRANCISCO

First Edition

ISBN
978-1-59780-073-0 (Trade Hardcover)
978-1-59780-072-3 (Limited Edition)

Night Shade Books
http://www.nightshadebooks.com

For Daisy Mae.

ONE

Sanie has been hearing him for days, she thinks, once she tunes into his voice. He's been there all along, lost among the creaks and gasps and groans of the old house, indistinguishable from the whisper of a breeze blowing through a window crack, though he's not speaking in a whisper, just softly, like a man gentling a tearful child or waking a lover.

She's alone in the kitchen, sitting at a table covered in waxy material with a green floral pattern, drinking a Diet Pepsi, when she first notices the voice. Like the rest of the house, the country kitchen, its white paint gone the yellow of an old document, is too spacious for what it contains. The twelve-foot ceiling dwarfs the appliances, making them seem like items from a kid's playhouse. A vintage stove and refrigerator that must date from the Forties. The 1940s, probably. Cabinets with glass fronts behind which rest jelly glasses and dishes that once were fine china, but now, their edges chipped, surfaces discolored, wouldn't fetch more than a nickel each in a yard sale. Taped to the refrigerator door is a Cumberland Farm Supplies 1977 calendar open to August, which happens to be the very month Sanie's living in thirty years later. The August illustration is a painting of a red-faced farmer on a red tractor in a freshly tilled field. He's wiping sweat from his brow with a bandana (also red) and his wife, a Playmate in gingham drag, looking artificially cheerful, a condition with which Sanie's all to familiar, is handing him up what appears to be a glass of lemonade. Sanie, who's feeling abandoned—Jackson, her husband, is studying for the bar and there's no one else around—is staring at this picture because it is significantly less dismal than the view out the window: under a driving rain, a corn field with last summer's stalks still standing, a demolished barn that's little more than a massive pile of kindling, and a fringe of woods. She's speculating on the farm wife's marriage, the quality of life in Cumberland Farm Supplies' Augustland, comparing her estimation of it to her own, and that's when the voice calls to her, softly, barely audible above the rain drumming on the roof, but distinct:

…Sanie… Sanie.

Startled, she turns to find the speaker, suspecting it's her husband. The idea she next entertains, that her mind is playing tricks, working up ambient noise into repetitions of her name, as sometimes happens when she's listening to car tires droning on a highway… this explanation doesn't hold up, because when the voice speaks again, it's too articulate, the words too clearly stated:

…I wish you could see me, Sanie.

"Hey!" she says, coming to her feet. "Who's there? Where are you?"

…I wish you…

The words blend together, *Iwishhooo,* and fade into a breath.

It can't be her husband—the voice has a thick southern accent, and Jackson's accent, though once as thick, has long since been scrubbed away though exercise of will, by Harvard, and four years in New York City. She thinks it might be Will, her brother-in-law, trying to spook her. There may be a secret passage and he's standing behind a hidden door, laughing at her. The Bullard house was built in the late eighteenth century—they were into secret doors and passages back then—and Will's weird enough to be playing such a game. He keeps a journal in which everything is written backwards. Peyote is his drug of choice. Thirty-six years old, he lives on a trickle of an inheritance, spends his time wandering in the woods, watching old horror movies, and reading magazines that feature histrionic articles about demonic possession, conspiracies between the Vatican and the Kennedy Administration, and how to survive the coming apocalypse. She's almost convinced that it is Will, but then recalls he had a doctor's appointment. It's too deep to be a woman's voice, so it can't be her sister-in-law, Louise, who is every bit as off-center as Will. Six years older and thus farther along the road to absolute weirdness. Sanie decides that the voice must have been her imagination.

Or maybe it's a ghost.

If ever a house deserved a ghost, it's this derelict antebellum mansion. A three-story home that might be featured in the real estate section of *The Astral Times*. Boards weathered to the brown of cured tobacco. The place is Cobweb Central, the last paint job done sometime during the Kennedy Administration. Shingles litter the weedy front lawn. Torn rusted screens on the porch. Steps missing and certain of the floorboards, when you put your weight on them, groan sharply as if you're stepping on a cat. Filled with three hundred years of eccentric accumulation. Permanently fogged mirrors. Every room a freak scene. Eminently Hauntable, the ad would read, with hot and cold running ectoplasm.

She toys with the idea of going into the study and telling Jackson she's seen… No, not seen. Heard a ghost. What's the point, though? She knows how he'd react. Without lifting his head from his book, he'd say, Yeah? and keep reading. If she were to persist, he would remind her sternly that ghosts do not exist, and if she continued to plead the case, he would say, Are you serious? Didn't ghosts go out with hippies? and give her a pitying look. She wonders how he came to be kin to Will and Louise. He's so straight, so completely un-weird, it's like he's a changeling. Or else, being the youngest, noting the unhappy consequences of Will-and-Louise's behavior, he has channeled his own weirdness into the formation of a clever disguise. Sometimes she finds herself wishing he was more like his siblings. A few weeks back, talking to her mom, she floated the idea of leaving Jackson. You're crazy, her mom said. Jackson's a doll. To which Sanie replied, Uh-huh, a boring doll. Malibu Ken after the lobotomy. There followed the lecture entitled: Just Because You're Bored Doesn't Mean He's Boring. Implying that if Sanie had something to occupy her, she wouldn't be bored. Sanie was forced to admit that this may be true. Though she's been struggling to write, she hasn't made much progress and is close to giving up on that obsession. But she's twenty-eight years old and she does not want that challenge to take the form of resurrecting a marriage that's on the verge of becoming a lifestyle choice.

It might be time, her mom said, to think about children.

A couple of Sanie's friends have already gone down that road, substituting a child for a vital life, and though the children make them happy, Sanie understands the trap they've built for themselves, the one that'll snap shut after the children leave home and they're forced to take a hard look at their husbands.

If the voice proves to be a ghost, she tells herself, at least that won't be boring.

TWO

Like many people from North Carolina, Sanie considers most South Carolinians to be either snooty and pretentious (Charleston types) or low-class and ignorant (the rest). The irony attaching to this point of view is not lost on her, yet she adheres to it, and the next morning, in keeping with her attitude, she wriggles into a pair of cut-offs and a raggedy T-shirt, Daisy Duke redneck-slut drag, prior to walking to Snade's Corners, a general store and gas station that lies at the end of the dirt road leading to the house. She means to engage the citizenry in visual terms to which they can relate and thus bridge the cultural divide. She seeks to infiltrate, to access secret hick lore that may come in handy for the grad-level creative writing workshop she intends to take once she and Jackson return to Chapel Hill. But either her disguise is ineffective or some behavioral tic gives her away, because when she reaches the store—a one-story structure of brown-painted boards, with a peaked roof that extends out over the gas pumps—and steps to the counter to pay for her Diet Pepsi, the cashier, a thirtyish, prematurely balding lout with a potbelly the size of a watermelon and a face remarkable only for an unfortunate Fu Manchu mustache and soul patch, says, "You Jackson Bullard's wife, ain'tcha?"

Sanie acknowledges this is the case, though she hates

the name Bullard. Sanie Bullard sounds to her like the name of a character in a story by a writer whom she would not admire, a faux-Southern regionalist with a faintly malodorous literary cachet.

"Your first time down, huh?" says the lout, first introducing himself as Garland Snade ("Gar's what they call me."), which sounds like a character from the same story. She tells him her name and he grunts a laugh, calls out to a teenage boy who's restocking one of the aisles: "Says her name's Zany Bullard!"

The teenager's doltish laugh calls to mind the word "guffaw."

"Sorry 'bout that," Gar says, mightily pleased with his own wit. "But I just couldn't resist. Thing is, the Bullards been a joke 'round Culliver County for years now. Not that that's any of your doing… or Jackson's, neither. Ol' Jackson, he tore out of town minute he could get a wheel under his butt. I hear tell he's done all right."

Much as she's inclined to, Sanie raises no objection to being lumped in with "you Bullards," and attests that Jackson is well on his way to world domination. Having made a small fortune as a day trader, he's embarking on a political career.

"Just like his daddy," Gar says. "Though if you was to ask me, it's Louise and Will who most take after ol' Rayfield."

Since Jackson never reminisces about his family, speaking of them solely in regard to practical matters, all Sanie knows about Rayfield Bullard is that he was a lawyer and is dead.

"Rayfield was a curious fellow," says Gar, responding to her inquiry. "Powerful man down at the State House for more than twenty years. Got to where people said you couldn't be governor unless Rayfield Bullard approved of you. Then his daddy died and left him the property, and Rayfield give up politics, his practice... just flat up and chucked the whole mess and come home to live. I reckon his wife dying not long before unsettled him some, and he just didn't want to deal with that mess in Colombia anymore. My daddy said a month or two after he arrived, he walked into the store and put in an order for enough baked beans to start a swamp fire. Beans and bread. That's all he ever bought. People hardly saw him after that. Man stayed to home and did whatever it was he did. Had most everything delivered. When he ventured out, you never knew what he'd do. It's like the man went strange the second he took over that house. I remember one time when I was a kid, he busts into the store wearing nothing but four hats, one on top of the other. Bought a Sunday paper, a couple quarts of beer, and said 'How ye doin?' to everyone, then stepped off right smartly down the road."

A new customer distracts Gar. Sanie goes out onto the porch with her soda, sits in a rusting lawn chair beside the door, and looks off along State Road 226, an asphalt straightaway laid between stands of scrub pine and palmettos, the foliage showing a leached green under the whitish sun. The smell is of hot dust and gasoline. Sweat trickles from her underarm and turns cool on the slope of her breast. A car zips by so swiftly, she can only make out a pasty blur at the wheel.

Is Jackson's fate, she wonders, to be the same as Rayfield's? A lifetime of sturdy labor and acquisition curtailed by a sudden swerve, a U-turn, as if he has stretched the elastic connection between himself and his home to a point at which he can no longer withstand its pull? An existence fueled by baked beans and accompanied by the wearing of multiple hats offers even less appeal to Sanie than the current strictures of the marriage. Could the ghost, the voice she hears, have something to do with the Bullard family character? She's heard it on three separate occasions now, she's become attuned to that mild baritone, and it troubles her that she's not more alarmed by the possibility of such a presence. Fear should be playing icy xylophone tunes along her vertebrae. She should be pleading with Jackson to flee from supernatural peril before it's too late. But whether due to ignorance or indifference, or because the presence communicates a certain familiarity, a non-threatening vibe, she's unafraid. The house has changed in her eyes from a monstrosity into a frail, musty puzzle that she wants to solve. There is, she imagines, a delicacy of purpose in the voice. Nothing sinister, merely a clever, cajoling sensibility. She expects that if a solution to the puzzle exists, it will be something redolent of lace and lilac water and a streak of crimson, an arrangement of color and texture that suggests some minor two-hundred-year-old violence that failed to meet the mark of tragedy. Still, she needs another perspective. Tonight, she decides, she'll tell Jackson, she'll ignore his predictable responses and make him reveal what, if anything, he knows.

A bicycle bell, insistently rung, brakes her train of thought. In front of the porch, sitting astride a bike, one leg braced on the ground, is a skinny towheaded kid, nine or ten years old, in jeans and a Gamecocks T-shirt. He stares at her with glum intensity and asks, "You Miz Bullard?"

Again, Sanie wants to deny it. "That's right. Who're you?"

"Sandy Kyle."

She waits a couple of beats for him to state his purpose, then says, "Something I can do for you, Sandy?"

"I want my cat," he says defiantly.

"You think I've got your cat?"

"Your brother Will took him."

"Will's my brother-in-law, not my brother. What makes you say he took your cat."

"'Cause I saw him. My cat was on y'all's porch and Will opened up the door and let her in. That was three days ago. I ain't seen her since."

"Why don't you ask him about it?"

Sandy toes up dirt, gazing down at the damage he's doing. "You gonna see him, ain'tcha?"

"Yeah, but you could ride on down there now."

Sandy seems uncomfortable with the idea. "I'm not in no hurry."

"You scared of Will? Is that what's wrong?"

"Heck, no! I talk to Will all the time."

"Well, then… go on down. I'm sure he's at home."

Sandy develops a look of woeful confusion, and Sanie suspects that he's experiencing one of those terrible, inexpressible conflicts between potential loss of face and personal mythology that children believe afflict only them.

"Okay," she says. "What I bet happened, Will let your cat in, then forgot about it. He's liable to forget his head, he isn't wearing his hat. And now she's wandering around, getting fat on our mice. What's she's look like?"

"She's a marmalade cat. You wanna yell out, her name's Kissy." A pause, then Sandy adopts a stern expression. "It was my mom named her."

Sanie tells him she'll do her best to find Kissy and, since Sandy's reluctant to disclose his phone number, says she'll leave word at the store. Walking home, she puts the cat issue on a back burner and thinks about the voice, the house, Jackson. After hearing Gar's story, she feels sorry for Jackson, and that makes her feel guilty about the thoughts she's been having regarding the marriage. Growing up a Bullard must be what caused him to become such a tight-ass. Maybe that's how his daddy was, rigid and orderly until the day his elastic band snapped him back to the ancestral stomping grounds.

She rounds a curve and the house emerges from behind the screen of two water oaks, ramshackle and many-eyed with black windows, presenting the impression of a ditsy old matriarch, her torso rising from waist-high yellowing weeds of skirts so ragged, the corroded wrought-iron fence of her bustle shows through. The weathered brown of the boards is identical to the skin tone of a mummy that Sanie remembers from a traveling exhibition of Egyptian artifacts in Raleigh. It's hard to imagine the place during its heyday, with white paint and lanterns lit and coaches drawn up along the road, begowned belles dancing the quadrille in the arms of gentlemen wearing frock coats and muttonchop whiskers. But that's how it was. The Bullards were gentry and, despite disapproving of his family, Jackson remains inordinately proud of the fact that one of his great-grandaunts many times removed married General "Light Horse" Harry Lee, who was Robert E. Lee's cousin or uncle or something.

Weeds tickle Sanie's thighs as she pushes in through the gate. A gust of wind flaps a torn porch screen. The steps creak shrill and feeble, like grandmothers complaining about their arthritis. The knockerless door has a deeper, more despairing voice, and the smells of two hundred years distilled into a musky cool breath rush to enclose her.

…I been wanting… I been waiting…

Anxiety bristles up in her, but she also feels a mild burst

of affection for the voice, and she thinks she detects a faint vibe of devotion, as if it's been waiting inside to squeeze out the cracked door, nearly tripping her up, and rub against her ankles.

THREE

Will's room on the third floor is, as Sanie's mama would say, a little slice of hell on earth. A cobwebbed chandelier with a single functioning light fixture. Hand-carved mahogany four-poster with stained, rumpled sheets. Two easy chairs upholstered in mauve velvet, worn shiny by generations of Bullard buttocks. Floor carpeted with magazines and newspapers, CD jewel cases, video cassettes sans sleeves, empty containers of the frozen dinners that Will heats in a microwave set atop his TV. Against one wall is his clean clothes pile. His dirty clothes are scattered about on the floor, a shabby archipelago lifting from the varicolored sea of magazines and newspapers. Will sits cross-legged amidst this chaos, spreading peanut butter on a peyote button. Pale and pudgy; neither handsome nor ugly, neutral in almost every aspect; he's a male version of his pale, pudgy sister, his shaggy, self-cut brown hair shorter by a few inches than hers, his face a study in concentration, as if dealing with the peyote button is taking all his energy. He's barefoot, wearing chinos and a brown polo shirt, and is the source of a strong unwashed odor. "Hi," he says, spotting Sanie standing in the hall.

She explains about the cat.

"Damn," he says. "Yeah, I gave her some milk and then got busy with something. I'll find her and put her out."

"Can you find her after taking that stuff?"

"I'll be able to see her, that's what you mean. Finding her's a whole other proposition."

Sanie supposes she should go hunt for the cat herself, but she's worn down from the heat, tired of having no one to talk with, so she flops into one of the easy chairs. "How come you're putting peanut butter on it?" she asks.

"The taste is fierce. I'm always looking for ways to make 'em taste better. Peanut butter's been working for me lately."

He pops the button into his mouth, screws up his face as he chews.

"How many you take at one time?" Sanie asks after he's done swallowing.

"Depends how big the buttons and your body weight. I did eight just now. That oughta be sufficient."

"What's it do for you?"

Will studies on this. "It lets me see stuff I can't see otherwise."

"What kinda stuff?"

"Only way you're gonna know is you take it yourself. 'Cause I tried to tell you, it'd sound stupid."

Though she's never tried anything of the sort before, Sanie has the urge to join Will on his psychotropic adventure, if only for the effect this would have on Jackson; but the urge fails to rise to the level of intent. Will goes to leafing through a magazine. It's odd how at ease she feels with him. With Jackson, there's rarely a moment when they sit together without talking. He attempts to manage the passage of their time, to use it to establish certainties between them, to have intelligent conversation… conversation that suits his notion of "intelligent." With Will, it's like they're two dogs who're used to the same run and have made all the essential accommodations. There's no stiffness, no sense of her feeling that she has to be any particular way. And yet she's known Will only a few days. Louise is a different matter. She's difficult to be around and, seeming to know this, she's hardly ever around.

"You feel it yet?" Sanie asks after several minutes, maybe ten, have elapsed.

"I got a queasy stomach. Colors are brighter. My thoughts are a little flippy."

"Sounds delightful."

"It gets better. Gets worse first, then it gets better."

Will's room is at the rear of the house, the windows opening onto the fields and woods. The sounds of passing cars are here inaudible. Just breezes and a hound baying in the distance. A blue jay chips at the stillness, then flies off, its wings flurrying, a flash of color past a window.

"How's Jackson doing with the books?" Will asks.

"I wouldn't know. He doesn't speak to me."

"He always was a bear for the books. Takes after Daddy that way."

Sanie's disturbed by the dissonance between this statement and Gar saying that Will and Louise took after Rayfield. "Think Jackson'll wind up like your daddy?"

"How you mean?"

"You know. Like he'll be going along, lawyering and all, then a screw'll come loose and he'll become an eccentric."

"I'm not sure I'd call Daddy eccentric. It was more like he just didn't give a damn what people thought about him anymore. He was kind of aggressive about it—he liked to shock 'em sometimes." Will's gaze sticks to a section of the wall, staring at—Sanie thinks—some newly brightened patch of color. "I suppose that in itself's eccentric to some.

But Daddy stayed sharp until the day he died. And he worked all the time, too. Same as Jackson."

"He was still lawyering?"

"No, he worked at whatever interested him. Genealogy for a while. Learned a bunch of languages so he could read books in the original. He retired is what happened. Being retired, he figured he could do what he wanted."

"So what about Jackson?"

"Will he wind up doing like Daddy? I couldn't tell you. Hell, this is the first time I seen Jackson in nine years. It bother you if he did?"

"Yes," Sanie says after considering her answer. "I don't doubt that it would."

"Well, if he is like Daddy, it won't be happening for a good while yet. Give you time to get used to the idea."

"I wonder… " Sanie doesn't finish the thought, unsure whether she should be so open with Will.

"What you wondering?"

"The thing you said about your daddy, him not caring anymore what people thought of him. You reckon Jackson's the same? That he's a lawyer because he needs people to think about him a certain way?"

Will ponders the question. "He didn't like being teased when he was a kid. For being a Bullard, y'know? I suppose a lot of what he's done is due to him hating that so much."

"Were you teased?"

"Oh, sure. Me and Louise rolled with it, though."

They grow quiet again, then Will says, "There some problem between you and Jackson?"

…Sanie… if I show myself to you, don't be afraid…

Will chuckles.

"What's so funny?" she asks,

"Nothing."

...Sanie... you won't, will you? You won't be afraid...

Will waves a hand at the air, giggles, and says, "Wow, man!"

"Did you hear that?" Sanie asks.

Will's expression grows pointed and, for the first time, she sees Jackson in him, how if you hollowed his cheeks and sharpened his features and painted him tan and gave him an expensive haircut and better clothes, you'd have a shorter, older Jackson.

"What did you hear?" he asks.

"A voice... a man's voice saying my name and stuff."

"My goodness. You can hear Wallace."

Suddenly suspicious that he's stoned and playing with her, she asks what he heard.

"Wallace was asking about if you were afraid."

"Wait! You... How's that possible?"

"It's nothing to be worried about. Ol' Wallace been hanging 'round since forever."

"We're talking about a ghost, right?"

"Can't think of much else he'd be."

"But you know him? You know who he is?"

"Not really. I went through some old albums, trying to find a face that matched the voice. I come across this guy named Wallace—that's all's written under the photograph is Wallace, so he must not have been part of the family. But he suited my conception."

"You live with a ghost and it doesn't bother you?"

"Don't seem to bother you that much."

Sanie acknowledges this with a halfhearted, "Guess that's true."

"He's not much of a ghost. It's not like he's scary. There's some cold spots, but no furniture moving or things floating up off the floor. All he does is say the same shit over and over, about him wanting you to see him. He never talks to you, just *at* you. He won't respond when you ask him something. And when you try and see him, when you say, Okay, let's do it, show yourself, it's like he loses interest."

"You tried, huh?"

"I walked all 'round the house for a coupla weeks, hoping he'd pop up, calling him out. Nothing. He comes back at me now and again, but basically the press is off."

"How come he knows my name?"

"He knows everybody's name. 'Least he knows everybody in the family. He doesn't manifest to anyone 'cept family."

"And you don't ever see him?"

"I don't believe there's anything to see. He's just a voice." Will belches, swallows hard; his expression becomes strained. "I might have to throw up soon."

Sanie, preparing to stand, says, "I'll get out of your hair."

"You can stick around if you want. I'm gonna go for a walk."

"I reckon maybe I better hunt for Kissy." Again she starts to stand, but is struck by a thought. "Those photograph albums… could I see 'em?"

"They're piled behind the TV. You want to check out Wallace, do you?"

"If it's all right?"

"Makes me no nevermind." Will struggles to his feet, sways, and says, "Whoa!"

Sanie asks if he needs help, suggests that he might be better off staying put; she'll look at the albums later.

Will moves unsteadily toward the open door, loose pieces

of paper adhering to the soles of his bare feet. "I'll be fine once I get this poison out of me." He pauses with one hand on the doorframe. A look of goofy transcendence—that's how Sanie characterizes it—comes to his face. She thinks he's about to speak, to bear illumined witness to some large and newly perceived truth.

"Need sunlight," he says, and is gone.

FOUR

To Sanie, everyone in the albums resembles a ghost. The gray, grainy photographs appear to have been shot through a particulate gauze of time, and the people, mainly nineteenth century types, seem captured while they were straining to hold their shapes, an instant before winking out of existence. Wallace proves to be a chunky teenage lad dressed in Confederate gray, a stressed expression tightening his fleshy face. Trying to act soldierly for the camera. He doesn't suit Sanie's image of the man whose voice she's hearing. She thinks that if Wallace were alive today, he'd be a high school nerd and spend hours playing role games on his computer. Until now, she's had no mental image of the voice's owner, but confronted by such a surfeit of images, she contrives one. Good-looking, though not stark raving handsome like Jackson. Kind of a cross between Jackson and Will, but more rugged than both. Outdoorsy. A gentleman farmer with an eye for the ladies. She wishes he'd talk to her again and, hoping to start him up, she says, "Hey, you! I'd like to see you," even though, after consideration, she's not at all sure that seeing him is what she wants.

Leafing through the albums tires her, or maybe it's the heat, her depression. After replacing the albums, she walks down the hall to her bedroom for a nap. Sometime later, a couple of hours judging by the sun, Jackson wakes her with a kiss, his hand gathering her breast. Muddled, she makes a complaining noise, but he's insistent, fondling her, his erection pushing at her thigh, and, guilty over what she's been thinking, she lets him have his way. There's an instant when she feels a clinical passion, when what he's doing triggers the appropriate reactions, but once he's inside her, he says something, a shopworn endearment that switches her off. She hurries him with her hips and soon he emits a series of explosive grunts, his body stiffening, then collapsing atop her. Dazed by the exertion, by the sunlight streaming through the window, by the absence of love, she listens to his cursory pillow talk. How about they go to dinner tomorrow night? He's getting a grip on the material, he can use a break. Is she finding enough to do? He doesn't want her to be bored. Sure, she says. That's good to hear. Absolutely. The house is fascinating. He kisses her cheek and returns to his studies.

She can't think of anything worth getting up for and falls back asleep. She dreams that she and Jackson have become separated from one another at a football game and, after searching for him briefly, she strikes up a conversation with a beer vendor, who works for a covert government agency. Together they share an adventure, are chased by bad guys through the steam tunnels that run beneath the University of North Carolina, and almost make love. When she wakes, she's bewildered by the darkness and silence, and when she remembers where she is, she feels like crying.

…Sanie… why won't you see me? Won't you… won'tchooo…

"Beat it," she says, and goes into the bathroom to take a shower.

Every so often as she showers, she peeks from behind the plastic curtain to make certain no one's there. The stains on the sink look like dried blood. The naked light bulb has attracted a tiny moth. The linoleum, patterned with mildew, holds a greasy shine and reflections appear to be shifting about inside the cut-glass doorknob. It's while she's drying herself that she remembers the cat. Shit! She's becoming forgetful as a Bullard. She puts on clean shorts and one of Jackson's shirts, grabs the flashlight from the night table, and goes off to hunt for Kissy. She rounds a corner and the beam pins a ghostly figure in a blowsy lavender nightdress. A Louise sighting. Her sister-in-law's puffy face registers a comical degree of shock.

"Louise," Sanie says. "You seen an ol' orange… "

Before Sanie can say "… cat," Louise has darted into her room and shut the door.

Sanie knows that Louise can't help the way she behaves; she's almost certifiable, pitiful in her inability to cope with the world, with basic functions such as civility. Nevertheless, she's fed up with Louise treating her like a pariah and is tempted to call out, to say something that will engage Louise's native paranoia.

She proceeds along the hall, down the stairs to the second floor. She half-whispers, half-hisses the cat's name; then, realizing that Will is hallucinating in the woods, Jackson can't possibly hear her, and Louise won't care, she calls out in her normal voice, "Kissy! C'mere, Kissy!" as she walks. The wiring on the first floor is sound and she flicks on the lights before entering the rooms. The switches for all the rooms are on the corridor wall. That you would want to light a room before opening the door speaks, she thinks, both to an exceptionally high level of anxiety and a consistency of trust that some mischievous soul won't flip the switch on while you're asleep. The vasty rooms are creepier with the lights on than they are in the dark. They have an air of having been suddenly vacated, as if the instant she hit the switch some shy, secretive thing vanished, leaving behind scarred furniture, ancient coffee tins filled with buttons and beads, and yellowed wallpaper with motifs of fleurs-de-lis and little woodland cottages and such, all evidences of its trite, irrelevant history.

The basement remains to be checked and Sanie's debating whether or not she wants to wait until morning to go down those rickety stairs, when she hears a *miaow* from the kitchen. She peeked into the kitchen earlier and could have sworn it was empty of cats. Another *miaow*. Kissy must have been behind something, under something. She switches on the light and pushes in through the swinging door and spots a tubby marmalade cat walking beneath the table, rubbing against chair legs, making demands for attention.

"Damn, girl," Sanie says, hoisting Kissy. "You might want to think about skipping desserts for a coupla weeks."

...Sanie... can you see me?

Though she's been expecting to hear the voice, it startles her nonetheless. Kissy doesn't appear to have noticed anything. She's purring, kneading Sanie's breast.

...I'm here... Sanie...

"Who are you?"

Kissy *miaows* again. Sanie absently strokes her. She repeats her question.

...You have to look close if you want to see. If you look close, yoooo...

Will said the voice never responded to questions, but that, she believes, might have been a response.

...close, Sanie...

Sanie looks, trying to scry out a glimmering against the yellow walls, a shadow with no source, a faint disturbance in the air, the slightest incidence of the supernatural. Kissy nips her thumb and she gives the cat a spank.

"Where do I look?"

…Sanie…

The voice has grown weaker and, frustrated, Sanie calls out, "Who are you?"

With a sudden twist, Kissy twists free of her arms and leaps to the floor, trots over to the wall beside the refrigerator, stands on her hind legs and begins pawing at the wall and *miaowing*. Sanie stares at the spot the cat is pawing and imagines that the yellow surface is, for a fraction of a second, shinier than it ought to be. But that's proof of nothing, and even if it were, it's not proof she's after. She isn't certain what she is after, yet as she watches the cat, who has given up pawing and is rubbing against the refrigerator, she thinks she might like to know one thing that makes no sense, that fits into no scheme, that aligns with no purpose, an irrational product whose existence would invalidate her every understanding of the world.

. . .

Jackson retracts his promise of an evening out; he's concluded that his grasp of contract law is not what it should be. He apologizes, promises to make it up to Sanie, but she's not disappointed, though she pretends to be. At dusk, she drives the cat down to Snade's Corners, this according to the contract she's entered into with Sandy Kyle. He's waiting with his mom, a fat woman with peroxide-blond hair who sits behind the wheel of a blue SUV, staring at a gas pump, refusing to acknowledge

Sanie. After examining Kissy—for signs of Bullardesque interference, no doubt—Sandy says, "Thanks," and scurries back to the SUV. Off they go eastward along State Road 226. Sanie's got half a mind to follow them, to catch onto the interstate and head for Myrtle Beach, find a happening bar and fuck the brains out of the first man she meets who doesn't engage her gag reflex. If such a man exists. It's been a long while, since she felt attracted to anyone, which is why the thought appeals to her. One of her friends, the proud mommy of a two-year-old son, says she hasn't wanted sex since the kid was born. Sanie feels the same way, yet has no childbirth trauma to explain it. She's afraid that giving up on that part of life will cause her to give up on everything.

She buys a tall can of Bud, neatly fitted into a paper sack, and sits drinking it on the porch, watching the land melt down into the dark. Snade's porch lights are on and moths whirl about the bulbs. The gas pumps gleam like robotic sentries. Male laughter from within, a caucus of bubbas by the cash register. She wishes she hadn't worn cut-offs… though if she wore jeans or slacks, she doubts Gar would be as solicitous. The screen door bangs open. A man steps onto the porch and takes a seat in the chair on the opposite side of the door. She hears the click of a cigarette lighter and, as if that sound has brightened her senses, the sawing of crickets intensifies in among the scrub.

"How y'all doing?" he asks.

"'Bout the way it looks."

His voice is nice—quiet and low, a little gravel in it. But if he says something on the order of, Well, if you feel like you look, you must be feeling beautiful, then she won't even bother to check him out.

"I guess you must be bored, then," he says. "Bored's

damn near an epidemic in Culliver County."

She puts him at a couple of years older than Jackson, in his mid-thirties. He's a couple of inches taller, too. Heavier through the shoulders and chest. Less a handsome face than a strong one. Thick brown hair tied off in a ponytail. There's grease on his hands, his face, and he's wearing a mechanic's jumpsuit, also grease-stained.

"So you're bored, are you?" she asks.

"I expect I'll get there 'fore long, but not just yet."

He takes a hit of his cigarette, tips back his head and exhales. His smoke collects about the light bulbs.

Sanie asks, "You a mechanic?"

"I own a collision shop over in Edenburg."

A silence settles between them.

"So what's there to do around here?" she asks.

"You're doing it." He points to her beer. "Me, soon as I wash up, I'll be attempting to play some music while I drink."

"Music? You mean like with a band?"

He chuckles. "Just barely. Bunch of us get together at a roadhouse up toward Edenburg every weekend."

"God, is it the weekend? I've lost track."

"Friday night. Hard to keep the days straight in these parts unless you got an engagement. It's not like anything much changes. Maybe a few more drunks on the road."

"What's your band called?"

"Local Prophet, Junior." He gives her an apologetic look. "The lead singer's got delusions of grandeur. It's a jam band, really. I only do it to keep my hand in."

"You were a musician before you owned the collision shop?"

"I did session work in LA for about ten years… 'til about three years ago."

"You moved here from LA? What's wrong with you?"

"LA wasn't working out."

"I'm sorry. I didn't mean to…"

"It's all right. Perfectly understandable. You gotta be crazy to migrate to a place like this. 'Course I grew up here, so that makes me doubly crazy." He grins at her. "What's your excuse?"

"My husband grew up here, too. We live in Chapel Hill, but we came back so he could have some peace and quiet while he's studying for the bar."

Disappointment flickers in his face when she says, "My husband…" but he covers it. "Peace and quiet's our chief resource. He should do real well." He hits his cigarette again. "He gets tired of studying, bring him down tonight. I'll buy y'all a beer."

"I'll tell him, but he's pretty locked in."

"And that's why you're bored, huh?"

"It's some of it." Sanie sips her beer. "But it's not all boring. We got ourselves a ghost."

"You serious?"

She tells him about the voice, the cat, what her brother-in-law Will said.

"This Will Bullard you talking about?" he asks.

She nods. "I suppose now you're gonna think I'm one of the crazy Bullards."

"Will's got some distances in him, but he's an okay guy."

"How you know Will?"

"He's been in the shop. Man's always getting into fender-benders." He flips his cigarette off to the side of the store. "I believe he mentioned something about a ghost one time. He said he saw it and…" He shakes his head. "I can't recall all what he said."

"That's funny. He told me he'd never seen it."

He waggles a forefinger. "I remember now. He said he was stoned and caught a glimpse of it. He was taking acid, I think."

"Peyote's more likely. He say what it looked like?"

"Tell you the truth, I was so busy ragging him about not being the most reliable witness, what with him being trashed, I didn't pay much attention."

Sanie sips her beer. "Maybe he was trying not to scare me—that's why he said he didn't see it."

"I suppose that's possible. Will's a gentle soul." He pushes up from the chair. "Well, I need to get washed up 'fore I go make a fool of myself." He offers his hand and says, "I'm Frank Dean."

"Sanie," she says.

"Pleased to meetcha."

He turns to go down the steps and she says, "Better tell me the name of that roadhouse. Y'know, 'case we can make it."

"The Boogie Shack. You drive toward Edenburg, you can't miss it. Got a big neon sign." He stands with one foot on the steps, one on the porch. "I wish you could see us play, Sanie. Be nice to have a new face in the audience."

It's not until he's gone that she realizes how closely his voice resembled the ghost voice she's been hearing... especially when he said, "I wish you could see us play, Sanie," which was so reminiscent in substance of what the ghost has been saying. She toys with the idea that he might have been a visitation, but ghosts don't drive black panel vans and leave cigarette butts lying in the gravel next to Snade's Corners. The thing that concerns her is what she was doing asking him so many questions. You're a musician? And you're in a band? Flirting with all the sophistication of a high school sophomore. God! Did she flutter her eyelashes? Yet she's pleased that she felt an attraction, even a mild one, though she's not sure she didn't talk herself into it, given the temperature of her thoughts before Frank Dean came out onto the porch. In the end she decides that what matters is she felt a tickle, a chemical whisper that proves she's not a ghost, not yet reduced to a sliver of instinct and emotion. It's something she can warm her hands over until she makes a more significant decision. She nurses her beer, delighting in the heat, the crickets going crazy out in the darkness beyond the gas pumps, headlights passing with beastly roars, the sheen of sweat on her thighs, luxuriating in these sensory treasures as if newly opened to them. She toys with the thought of driving to the Boogie Shack. The Boogie Shack, for God's sake! Down here it's like the Doobie Brothers never went away. Like Steppenwolf is still riding high on the charts. She won't go. It's not in her to take that risk, but she enjoys tempting herself, imagining how it would be to walk into the place and stake out a barstool, the air conditioning cool as nirvana after the swampy night air, the two-legged flies starting to circle, beer ads glowing red and haloed like Satan breathed out smoke rings made of Hell's finest Havana and they hardened into words and logos… She cuts this vision short, knowing that if she indulges in it much longer, she'll begin to question what she's risking by not taking such a risk.

FIVE

Sanie's in a mood all the next day. Will annoys her. Louise, whom she catches unawares in the kitchen, annoys her by blurting, "I'm sorry," and rushing out the back door. When she calls her best friend Brittany on her cell, Brittany annoys her by being too busy to talk. Jackson, in particular, annoys her. After she tells him about the ghostly voice, the cat, what Will and Frank Dean had to say, he takes off his reading glasses and gives her that reproving yet temperate Atticus Finch through-his-eyebrows look she once thought was sexy and says, "Frank Dean? You mean Frank Dean Irving? You were talking to him?"

"I don't know about Frank Dean *Irving,*" she says. "Frank Dean's all he told me.'

"That's what everybody calls him. Like Tommy Joe. Billy Bob. He was a few years ahead of me in school. The guy was an egomaniac. He thought he was a rock star because he played in some ridiculous band."

"Well, I guess he *was* a rock star."

She tells him about Frank Dean's session work in LA.

"What's he doing now?" Jackson asks.

"He owns a collision shop in Edenburg."

"Some rock star." Jackson puts his glasses back on. "You watch yourself. The guy's a hound."

Hound, she thinks. Back in Chapel Hill, Jackson

would have used a more decorous term. Ladies man or womanizer. He must be getting in touch with his roots.

"So you're suggesting that I need to be more restrained in my behavior? My natural sluttishness puts me at peril?"

He turns to his book. "I'm saying you don't want to give a guy like Frank Dean the wrong impression. And all it takes to give the wrong impression is you talking to him."

She's standing in the doorway of the study, Rayfield's study, the walls lined with shelves holding law books, paperbacks, and what appears to be a lifelong collection of *National Geographic*s. The desk is brown wood, the chairs are brown leather, the rug is mostly brown with a delicate yellow Mexican pattern, even the air is brown. Thus it follows, she thinks, that Rayfield must have been brown, a brown soul suited in a lawyer's pin-striped serge. It's a color Jackson seems to be growing into. Though she's guilty at having flirted, she hates him for making her feel the guilt. He knows as well as she that they're in trouble, yet he refuses to acknowledge it; he wants everything to be according to plan. Wife, profession, house, children. Bumpity bumpity bump. She doesn't believe she should have to feel guilty over desiring to escape what he would desire to escape if he allowed himself to take stock emotionally, to understand what they're becoming.

"What about the rest of it?" she asks.

"The rest of what?"

"What I told you."

He sets down his book. "Put yourself in my shoes, okay? I'm studying for the bar. I'm under…"

"I'm aware you're studying!"

"… under a hell of a lot of pressure. I'm striving to get myself into a position where I can upgrade our lives. And my bored-shitless wife comes in and tells me she's having

Steven King moments… an experience seconded by my crazy brother and an asshole I haven't seen since high school. How would you react?"

"I'd assume my wife wasn't delusional. That there might be a problem."

"Well, that's you. Me, I assume there's no problem here that warrants abandoning my responsibilities. But that's because I actually *have* responsibilities."

His voice is strained. It's as angry as he ever gets, and she wants to let her own anger out, to make him understand exactly where his responsibilities lie and how badly he's failing them, how he can do nothing other than fail them, but she knows where this will lead.

"Fine," she says. "Why don't I just leave you, then?"

A puzzled expression. "What?"

"I said why don't I just leave you to 'em. Your awesome responsibilities. That be all right?"

She stalks off into the hall, momentarily satisfied by this small venomous triumph, but stops outside the door and has to fight back tears. What in God's name, she asks herself, is holding her here? A vague sense of purpose moves her away from the door, but whatever the purpose is remains unclear. She wanders downstairs and, as usually happens when she wanders, winds up at the kitchen table, staring at the calendar picture of the farmer and his wife. There is, she realizes, a strong proletarian influence in the picture. The red tractor, the farmer's brawny arms, the honest sweat on his brow, the wife's earnestness in servicing his thirst: with a more rigorous line, it could pass for Soviet poster art.

She assigns herself a project: Explore What Has Gone Wrong. It's a project she's attempted before, always with the same indefinite result, but this time, maybe, she'll see something new. One by one, she examines the assumptions she made when she agreed to marry Jackson. Did they represent basic misunderstandings or has he changed? Has she? If they've changed, there may be hope that they can change again. Was his intellect vivid, as she once thought, or dronelike, as she thinks now? Were his witticisms originally so standardized, so programmed? Did his good looks have the lifelessness of a male catalogue model the day she spotted him in the student cafeteria? It's an impossible task, and part of its impossibility lies in the fact that she doesn't care what the answers to these questions are. And whose fault is that? her mom would ask. Sanie's never been able to answer that question to her own satisfaction, but now she believes she could. Nobody's, she'd say. Everybody's. Fault is in the air.

...Sanie...

"Go away," she says.

"Sanie?"

"Leave me alone!"

Footsteps behind her and she swivels her head about. Will, dressed as for church in a baggy gray suit and foulard tie, standing bewildered by the door.

"Something wrong?" he asks.

"What do you want?"

"I'm going into Edenburg for the day. You need anything?"

Valium. A shotgun. A one-way ticket to Madagascar.

"A coffeemaker," she says. "And some decent coffee."

It's a test. Assign a task and see if it gets done. If he performs in typical Bullard style, she'll end up buying it herself.

Will looks buffaloed. "You want me to buy a coffeemaker?"

"I can't stand another cup of instant."

"How much are they?"

"Jesus Christ, Will! I'll pay you back. Don't worry about it."

"I was just wondering. I never bought one and I don't want to get screwed on the price."

"Is there a drugstore in Edenburg?"

"Yeah, sure. They got everything there."

"Go to the drugstore. Buy a coffeemaker. Shouldn't cost more than twenty or thirty bucks. Whatever it costs, buy it. Then go to the supermarket and pick up some French Roast coffee. Make sure it's the kind that works with the coffeemaker. Can you handle that?"

"You don't have to be pissy."

"Sorry." To soften the atmosphere, she asks why he's all dressed up.

"Going to the movies. I got a date."

Woe betide. Another generation of Bullards in the offing.

"Who's the girl?"

"She works in the bakery at the Piggly Wiggly."

The scheme of Will's life seems to sketch itself out before her, asymmetrical and haphazard, full of odd knots and interconnections, like a web woven by a schizophrenic spider.

"Y'all have fun now," she says,

"She's pretty. Not as pretty as you, but she's…" He appears to be struggling with a matter of degree.

"She does it for you," Sanie suggests.

"Yeah," he says, brightening. "Yeah. A lot."

"Well, y'all have a nice time."

Will hovers. "Her name's Allie. Short for Alexandra."

Sanie says, "Uh-huh."

"You want to meet her, I can ride you in some evening. She gets off at five. Actually, I could ride you in…"

"Will?"

"… Tuesday." He blinks rapidly. "What?"

"This isn't a good time right now."

"Oh." He backs up as if warned away from a poisonous snake and bumps against the door. "Okay. I'm… I'll go."

"I'll talk to you later."

"Sanie?"

"Yes."

Will's hands fumble with the air as if he's trying to describe female curves, then he says, "I wish there's a way to stop things you know are happening from happening."

Sanie understands from this that Will has noticed Jackson and her are having problems. "Things'll sort themselves out," she says,

"I know. That's what Louise tells me, but I always get the urge to try and help."

Wanting to change the subject, she says, "How come Louise won't talk to me?"

"She don't like talking to people. She's been like that forever."

"She talks to you. I've even seen her say a few words to Jackson."

Will's jowly face droops, acquiring a morose expression better suited to the face of cartoon dog. "I don't reckon she thinks of us as people."

SIX

Almost all the magazines littering Will's room, to which Sanie retreats in midafternoon, contain articles about ghosts. They speak of cold spots, horrid noises, blood weeping from ceilings, flowers withered by the touch of immaterial fingers, messages that fade from notepaper, harridans with gory knives and skeleton grins, soldiers on insubstantial steeds, but nowhere a mention of a barely audible voice that tends to repeat itself again and again, a few simple phrases and their variants. Perhaps such a minimal presence falls beneath the notice of magazines— more spectacular phantoms are their stock-in-trade. Or perhaps the voice is atypical of lost souls. She's curious why Will has so many articles dealing with ghosts. Has he researched the subject? Does he, as Frank Dean implied, know more than he's telling about what's going on in the house? Unable to provide answers to these questions, Sanie's interest flags. She dozes in a velvet chair and wakes to hear Jackson calling to her. Knowing he wants food, sex, beer, laundry, or something fetched from town, she tiptoes to the door and shuts it. It's coming on dusk, the fields dissolving in carbon-colored gloom. She observes the process distantly, standing at the window and half-listening to Jackson. Once he stops shouting, she sneaks down the stairs and out the front door and walks briskly through the buzzing, stifling dark toward Snade's Corners. The store's becoming a sanctuary, a place where she feels detached from the marriage, from the Bullards and their dysfunction.

She's walking the curve between Snade's and the house, when she hears a car behind her and moves onto the shoulder. Headlights saw across the shrubs on the opposite side of the road. Then the car is on her, its black flank swerving past inches from her hip. An eerie, alarming passage, like a shark's fin surfacing by your shoulder as you're treading water. She stumbles back, catches her heel, and goes sprawling in the roadside ditch. The car, a black panel van, brakes hard and a man calls, "You okay?" Stunned, she comes to all fours. Her left knee is stinging and her heart's doing a trance beat. A hand snags her arm, helps her to stand.

"Sanie… Jesus! You okay?"

Frank Dean. His face etched with worry.

She wrenches free of his grip. "Whyn't you look where you're going? You could have killed me!"

"I'm sorry. You were in the blind spot. There's a blind spot covers about ten, fifteen feet of the curve. You were right in it."

"You think maybe you should take that into account when you're driving? God!"

"I'm sorry! I really am!"

He tries to take her arm again and she swats at him. "Leave me be!"

"You're bleeding."

Her left knee and shin are shiny with blood. The sight makes her shaky. "Fuck!"

"I'll drive you home so you can get that bandaged."

Her head swims. She's willing to accept the ride, but

thinks of Jackson, how he'll react. "No! They don't have bandages, they don't have anything there!"

It's a lie, but saying this brings her to the edge of tears, as if she's touched on a sadder, more telling lack.

"We'll fix you up at Snade's, then," Frank Dean says. "Come on."

He steers her to the passenger door, tells her there's Kleenex in the glove compartment. As he drives, she dabs at her knee, soaking up the blood, exposing a contusion below her kneecap. She must have fallen on a rock. Queasy, she leans back and squeezes her eyes shut.

At the store Frank Dean sits her down on a porch chair and hurries inside. Sitting calms her. The grease-smeared concrete apron, the gas pumps, and moth-flurried light bulbs are persuasive in their ordinary solidity. They do not threaten to yield spectral voices. He returns with iodine, bandages, rubbing alcohol, and kneels before her, as if intending to treat her himself. She tells him she can do it. As she cleans the leg, he sits on the top step, continuing to apologize. He's wearing jeans and a different Hawaiian shirt. Dressed for the Boogie Shack. The screen door opens and Gar emerges. The porch lights polish his high forehead to a pinkish glare, causing his Fu Manchu to look even more ridiculous than usual.

"Had yourself an accident, didja?" he says.

"I cut myself shaving," Sanie says, feeling intruded upon.

Gar doesn't appear to notice her attitude. He puts his hands on hips, sticks out his belly. "Pretty nasty cut there."

"Really? You think?" Sanie applies a cotton pad to the knee.

"'Pears like you making a habit of running down

females," Gar says to Frank Dean.

"Goddamn it, Gar! Don't you see she's shook up? Last thing she needs is you standing over her and gabbing."

"Excuse me! I was just trying to be friendly."

Gar retreats into the store and Sanie, taping the pad to her knee, asks, "What'd he mean by that?"

"About me running down females? It's not exactly a habit. My last girlfriend, way we met, she pulled out in front of me against a red light. Gar made a big deal out of it. He's a good shit, but he doesn't have a whole lot to do with himself."

Sanie finishes taping.

"You need aspirin, I got some in the van."

"Okay."

While he fetches the aspirin, she limps into the store and buys a tall Bud. Gar, along with two brothers in doofusness, is watching preseason football on a smallish TV behind the counter. She goes back onto the porch, gulps down the aspirin with a swallow of beer. Frank Dean retakes his seat on the steps.

"You must be a neighbor of ours," Sanie says. "Or isn't that where you live, down our road?"

"I don't know I'd call myself a neighbor. My place's about eight miles farther along." He pauses. "Feeling better now?"

"Much."

"I was worried there. You were looking pale."

"Almost getting run over tends to set me back a step."

A red station wagon slows on the highway and pulls up alongside the pumps. The driver, long-haired and bearded, rests an elbow in the window and says, "You might wanta get a move on, Frank Dean. We need to do a sound check." He gives Sanie the once-over and says, "Hi."

"Sanie," says Frank Dean. "This here's Ryan."
"Hey, Ryan."

Ryan offers her a wave that's half a salute. "No shit, man. I want the balance on the PA right. Couldn't nobody hear the vocals last night."

"I'll be along."

"Those guys from Myrtle Beach said they'd be there tonight for sure," Ryan says. "We do a good show, we might start making some real money. So let's be prepared, okay?"

"I'm right behind you."

Ryan looks doubtful. "Whyn't you bring her along? Maybe she'd like watching us setup."

"Just ease your egg bag, Ryan. I'm there."

"Is he the singer?" Sanie asks as Ryan pulls out onto the highway.

"He thinks he is." Frank Dean taps out a cigarette from a pack of American Spirits, but doesn't light up. "This band is history."

"Why do you say that?"

"'Cause the talent's all in the rhythm section and the only ones serious about the band are Ryan and the lead. Pretty soon we'll go to having these morbid discussions about commitment and the band's direction. We'll start having personal hassles. Y'know… Like who's carrying the load, who's getting the jobs, putting up flyers? That kinda thing. Before that happens, I'll find myself somebody else to jam with. I love music, but I've had it with the bullshit that goes with it." He hangs the cigarette behind his ear, a habit that's always appealed to Sanie, and stands. "I gotta go. You want to come along, you're welcome."

"I wish I could."

"You sure? I can run you back after the first set, you

want to go for a beer and a listen."

She's tempted, but says, no, she can't.

"Okay. Next time, maybe."

She stays on the porch for another beer after he's gone. Two farm boys are the only customers. They nod and say, "Evenin'." She regrets not having gone to the Boogie Shack with Frank Dean. It would have been a breach of regulation, but it's a regulation that seems wrongfully binding. The Boogie Shack would not gave been life-changing, probably not even entertaining, but she needs something to break the monotony. Drinking beer on the porch of Snade's Corners doesn't cut it. If she were motivated, she would return to the house and begin the process of narrowing down her career choices. She could jump back into grad school, or try that writing course. There is no end of challenging options, but it seems the challenges oppress her. What's missing from her life is life. Without its current pouring through her, she can't unlock her motivation. She's unable to comprehend how she reached this pass. How she became such a slug, a drudge. Though Jackson was a complicitor in her decline, she knows she let it happen. But she also knows that while her decline and that of the marriage have fed into each other, they don't run off the same battery. If she were suddenly to evolve into a dynamo, it would make her even less respectful of Jackson. She thinks it may be their co-dependency, their mutual slump into the ordinary, that has preserved the union.

She walks back to the house without much difficulty. The voice welcomes her home. She mocks it. "I wish I could see you, too," she says. "I'd kick your ass."

…Sanie… I wish…

"Yeah, you wish! Leave it to the Bullards to attract a

wimpy ghost."

In need of a Diet Pepsi, she goes into the kitchen. Jackson's at the table, a Heineken and a half-eaten sandwich on a plate before him.

"Hey!" she says, and makes for the refrigerator.

"What have you been up to?" he asks in an arch tone that is, she recognizes, an effort to hide surliness.

"Nothing. Sitting on the porch at the Corners. Drinking a beer." For punctuation, she pops open the Pepsi. "Couple cars passed, couple good ol' boys said 'Howdy.' That's about it."

"You were sitting on the porch at Snade's dressed like that?"

When did you get to be such a prude?, she wants to say. When did my behavior become so inappropriate?

"It's hot! What am I supposed to wear?"

"Did you hold up a sign saying Will Work For Beer?"

"What are you on about? You used to sit on the stoop drinking beer all the time."

"That was then, this is now."

"Yeah, been there, done that."

He gives her a perplexed look.

"I thought," she says, "you might want to communicate in slogans. Catchphrases. Y'know, in case we could arrive at a meeting of the minds that way. Like I'd say, 'When the going gets weird, the weird turn pro,' and then you'd go, 'Beauty fades, but stupid is forever.'"

"Are you drunk?"

"Shitfaced. I can barely stand. It's taking all my strength to maintain a pose of sobriety."

With a display of manly gusto, as if tearing at raw meat, he rips off a bite of sandwich and chews. "What happened to your leg?"

"If it's broke, you promise not to shoot me?"

He refuses to dignify this with response.

"I tripped," she says. "Walking to the Corners. I tripped and fell on my butt."

He takes another bite, makes a gruff noise that seems to convey his acceptance of the story. Under the glare of the overhead, the walls are the rancid yellow of spoiled custard. The refrigerator clicks and starts to hum.

"Aren't you going to sit down?" he asks.

"I was just waiting for an invite. Didn't want to interrupt the cramming." She pulls back a chair and plops into it.

"Maybe we should go back to Chapel Hill."

"Why's that?"

"I don't think you're doing well here."

And you thought I was doing well in Chapel Hill? "You said you couldn't study there."

"I can't… not with the phone ringing all the time."

When do you ever answer the phone? she thinks. "You don't have to take the calls," she says.

"If I'm there, yes, I do."

She's inclined to examine this logic, but understands that the childlike perversity that's inspired his statement won't profit from examination. "Rattling around in this house isn't my idea of a great time, but do what you need to. I'm fine."

"Let's see how it goes."

"Whatever. It's only until the end of November." She flashes a grin and adopts a tough quasi-masculine tone. "I can do that much time standing on my head."

The grin once served to disarm him, but it has no measurable effect now. Sober as a pickle, he stands and carries his book, beer, and plate toward the door.

"You ask me to sit down and then you leave?" she says.

"What's that about?"

"I just thought you should get off that leg."

But she knows that she failed to provide a backboard for his ego and so he's sulking off to the punishment room in hopes she'll feel sorry for him.

"I scraped my knee," she says. "It's not a torn ACL."

"Best not to take any chances," he says as an exit line.

She rolls the cold can of pop back and forth across her brow in an attempt to suppress the headache that's starting to build, but she realizes she'll need a stronger remedy.

SEVEN

…if only you could see me…

"I see you! All right?"

…Sanie…

"God, please go away! I'm trying to work."

I don't know what I'll do…

"Too bad shooting yourself isn't an option."

…Sanie… Sanie…

"You want me to read to you? I bet you do. Let me see here…"

…I wish yoooo…

"Now this is the first note I ever took. 'Start with an ant crawling beside a chain-link fence.' I don't have the slightest idea what that refers to. The context, y'know. It's gone. But I put it in the front of all my notebooks for luck. And this, too. 'On the last day of the world, the gargoyle changed from stone to flesh and just sat there.' That was an assignment Professor Demery gave us—to write a one-sentence story. I only got a C, but I liked it. Fact that the gargoyle sits there implies a lot about its upbringing. But Demery thought I was trying to be funny, which I suppose I was."

…Sanie…

"You hush! Let me see what else I got. Oh, here you go. This is another assignment. Demery told us to take a contemporary news story and sketch out a scene relating to it. I picked Katrina. That's the name of this big ol' hurricane that flooded New Orleans. So I put this guy, Harry, and his wife out front of their house. They just emerged after the storm, and there's this man wading down the street, who Harry talks to. Okay?

" ' "That was some fucking hurricane." Harry was standing atop a triangular chunk of cement that had been part of our house, gazing off across the desolation. "I mean, that wasn't no pissant tropical depression, that was a hurricane."'

" ' "Hey, there!" the man hollered. "Your house is unsafe!"'

" 'Harry glanced at me over his shoulder. "You believe this shit?" He turned back to the man. "Think I don't know that?"'

" ' "Authorities gonna come along and tell you it's unsafe!"'"

Sanie pauses, reads what follows silently. "This really, really sucks."

Silence.

"So what do you think?"

The silence continues.

She slaps the notebook down on the table.

"You go to hell!"

EIGHT

Three days later, when she comes into the kitchen, yawning and sleepy-eyed, Sanie finds a coffeemaker and a bag of French Roast on the counter. "Bless you, Will," she says. She's settling down with her first cup when the kitchen door is pushed inward and a pale, dark-haired woman in a red terrycloth robe walks in. "Oh," she says, stopping dead, a hand on her breast. Though prettier than might be expected, her aghast expression and anxious demeanor tell Sanie that this must be Will's girlfriend, likely the reason it took him three days to purchase a coffeemaker. Sanie offers a cup, fresh-made, and in a voice so frayed and fey, it sounds like a shaving left over from a Stevie Nicks vocal, the woman says, "Caffein's a poison. It'll rot your teeth worse than sugar." She remains stuck in the pose she struck on entering. "I didn't know anyone else would be up."

Sanie introduces herself.

"Hello," says the woman, and darts a glance to the side as if trying to locate a weapon, something she can use as a defense.

"You're Will's friend. Allie, is it?"

A nod.

It appears Will has found a woman who's every bit his equal in the area of social ineptitude. That's amazing in itself. The fact that she's attractive in a sweetly old-fashioned kind of way, with a cameo face and piled-up smokey brown hair… that's a miracle.

"So…" Sanie rots her teeth with a sip of hot caffein. "How'd you and Will get together?"

"It was fate," says Allie.

No further information seems to be forthcoming.

"Fate in the sense of a cosmic plan?" Sanie asks wryly. "Or more like an operation of chance?"

She's not expecting an answer, but Allie, deadpan, says, "The former, I believe. Will's very much in harmony with the cosmos 'cause of all the drugs he takes."

"Huh," says Sanie, dumfounded. "Wow."

"The drugs allow him to see things we can't."

Either Allie's putting her on, Sanie thinks, or else she's a cult convert, repeating what's she's been programmed to say by Swami Will. Or maybe it's love.

"I have to go," Allie says. "We're driving to the Meher Baba Center in Myrtle Beach. Do you know Baba?"

"Dead Indian guy, right? Religious figure?"

Allie's dismayed reaction is so profound, Sanie feels ashamed at having smart-mouthed her.

"I'm sorry," Sanie says. "I had a rough night. Come on, sit down. We can chat."

"Will says you're in danger."

Was that a glimmer of vindictiveness in Allie's face? Was the warning offered as a curse? Sanie thinks so, yet at the same time, it's hard to believe this Vegan redneck could have a mean zone in her astral body.

"Did he specify the nature of this danger?"

"Imminent," says Allie, pronouncing the word with a British precision. She marches toward the door.

"Did you come in here for a reason?" Sanie asks. "Something you needed, maybe?"

"Oh. Yes. A spoon."

"Top drawer left of the sink."

Allie pads over to the sink, extracts a spoon and, holding it in front of her like a nun holding a cross, exits without another word spoken. Sanie wonders what she'll do with the spoon. Bend it with her mental rays, maybe. Stir some herbal fungus into her yoghurt. Spank Will. It's best not to speculate. As for Will's warning—if it *was* his and not Allie taking a cheap shot at her for having dissed the avatar—she supposes it was a part of Will's love tactics, impressing Allie with his knowledge of the beyond so as to get her into the sack.

Jackson comes in for coffee, compliments her on the French Roast-coffeemaker parley. He's cheerful, all "what's your day looking like?" as if last night never happened. He's put the old blinders on again. The world lies straight ahead. Those dark barriers that delimit your vision, they're there to remind you of your course, not to hide the truth. Sanie's cheerful back at him. She can, by God, outcheerful his ass on her worst day. Today she goes for a Reese Witherspoon perkiness. Blissfully perky. Yesterday she expressed the cheerfulness of a bygone era, a cross between the Two Marys, Poppins and Tyler Moore. Will ducks his head in. He's off for the shore and won't return until evening. Can he bring them anything? Videos, Sanie says, insisting on no monsters, no demons, witches, or serial killers. That just-laid peppiness to which all men are prone manifests in him as a blithe good cheer, at odds with his typical somber mood. A tennis sweater knotted about his neck would be appropriate. Ta-ta, she expects him to say. She pictures him tooling away in an MG and not the thousand-dollar shitbox he drives. Jackson walks out with him, coffee in hand. The kitchen closes down around Sanie. Her normal level of depression settles in.

She drinks three more cups of coffee. The house, its silence accentuated by the burst of chatter, seems mournful, an enclosure given over to a timeworn grief. Something's missing, but she can't think what. Then she realizes that she hasn't heard the voice since the previous night. Maybe she's chased it away. This depresses her further. Though irritating, it has been her most reliable companion. If it comes back, she decides, she'll make a serious effort to grant its wish… which gives her an idea. A ridiculous idea, and yet it grows on her. After washing her coffee cup, she climbs the stairs and enters Will's room and pulls the cardboard box in which he keeps his peyote from beneath the bed. The neatly made bed. He's cleaned up, stacked his magazines and done some spotty dusting. Sitting on the bed, she contemplates the buttons. Little gray-green pincushions. Magic vegetables that allow one to see what no on else can. She debates the rationality of what she's considering. There's no debate, really. It's completely irrational. But irrationality appeals to her. The worst that can happen, she'll throw up.

Cautiously, as if picking up a hand grenade, she selects one of the buttons and—how awful can it be?—takes a bite. The taste is almost indescribable. Bitter at first, then the bitterness swelling into a flavor of pure corruption. She gags, stares at the pulpy rotten thing. The peanut butter is resting atop the microwave. She gets the jar and—as Will demonstrated—spreads peanut butter over the button until she's created a ball of peanut butter with a peyote center. The taste is manageable, albeit still vile. Over the course of the next fifteen minutes she succeeds in downing five buttons. That's the limit of her tolerance. Given that she's significantly lighter than Will, five should do the trick. The buttons are heavy in her stomach, like they've assembled into a sour revolting mass, and though she's not yet nauseous, she senses a potential for nausea. She sits in the chair closest to the window and waits.

The high comes on gradually. Time slows. Surfaces begin to glisten, the walls to billow slightly, like dark brown curtains on which a design of boards has been printed. Her heart rate's rapid, her neck muscles wired. Her stomach aches and feels bloated, causing her so much discomfort, she can't sit still, and yet she thinks it should be bothering her more than it does—there seems to be a disconnect between her brain and her stomach, and she's not getting the full effect. Her thoughts zoom erratically, spurts of perceptual acuity alternating with obsessive interludes. For a while she's persuaded that the other mauve velvet chair is turning into a mauve-colored man with his head slumped onto his chest and she speculates on what the chair will say upon waking to its new form. Something more than "Howdy," she reckons, and giggles. She has an impulse to switch on the TV, but its stored electricity tingles her fingertips, repelling her. A sweat breaks out all over her body. Shudders issue from some central place inside her. Her saliva production increases dramatically and the nausea intensifies. She's afraid she's going to throw up, then yearns to throw up, but she doesn't want to chance leaving the room and having Jackson see her. She must look awful. Wondering how she looks distracts her from her stomach trouble. She digs around and unearths a hand mirror streaked with traces of white powder. The face that stares back at her from the glass is that of a plague victim. Blotches of redness. Enormous pupils. Pores the size of BBs. The reflection fascinates her. She continues staring at it until she has the thought that staring at it is holding her back, retarding the drug's process. The mauve chair has evolved into an entity half man, half chair. The man's head is a knob of grayish blue bone, its single feature a crimson gash of a mouth. He's not real, or rather he's an emblem of reality, shorn of its customary disguise. Crystalline glints might be tiny swimmers in the air with diamond skins. In an upper corner of the room, a spiderweb pulses, an ashen lace membrane, and the corner itself, suddenly vast to her eyes, a vault of gloomy stone that hums with many voices in unison, their solemn electric harmony, a cathedral-choired corner... Sick again, violently so, she rushes to the window and vomits into the back yard. Even after she's emptied her stomach, she remains with her head hung out the window, eyes shut, too weak to move. Yellowjackets buzzing around their nest in the roofpeak sound like a squadron of approaching fighters. The warmth of the day is fractioned into dozens, hundreds of smells. Bitter grasses, fecal sweetnesses, the morose odor of the ancient wood, unnamable essences. The fields, formerly without pattern, now seem pattern's source, an infinity of mosaics layered one atop the other. Flows of grass, maps of stones and dirt, ideograms of twigs, equations of crumpled cans and paper trash. Meaning lies everywhere, decryptified. But meaning is not relevant to the bright flash of being that signals her through the world. The sun's godly heat soaks into her bones.

The purge, she realizes, is the secret of the high. Perhaps the secret of life. Voiding oneself of the poisons that limit the freedom to see, to know. Though she's foul with sweat, heart accelerated, stomach still not right, in a way she's never felt better, never more sighted, more attuned to the vibrations that, without notice, have been passing through her. She's not in complete control of her body.

She tends to list when she walks. Every step tremulous and new. But it's all good, an adventure. Tired of the room, its stale confine—Will's smells, too, have grown myriad and distinct—she goes out into the hallway, its diminishing perspective as undulant and unstable as the rest of creation. It's cooler here. Drier. Eddies in the air. Opaque disturbances. Gooseflesh spreads over her arms and legs. She tries to remember why she ate the peyote. Something she wanted. God, it's really getting cold! She hugs herself, shivers. The cold, she imagines, is a function of the drug. One of Will's shirts might help... if she can find one that's clean. She turns back toward Will's door and now she recalls why she did peyote. It's barely visible against the sunlit window at the far end of the hall, a wisp of a thing, like a painting on glass that's all but worn away, almost colorless: a young woman, portions of her jaw and cheek eroded, body erased below the knees, wearing a gown that retains a faint bluish tinge. And she's not alone. In a large spiderweb that spans between the ceiling and the top of a door, part of a man's bearded face has begun to accumulate, as if it's using the strands of the web for structure, so decrepit that it needs the structure in order to become tangible. Sanie's a little frightened, but only because what she's seeing is so strange. There's no inimical vibe attached to these apparitions. No grotesque displays, no ghastly sounds. The Bullard manse, it appears, is a warren for the sad and dissolute of the spirit world. Those are the colors of their haunting, the faded family colors. They materialize from every part of the hall, from old times not forgotten when Dixie wasn't merely a laughable conceit, but a place of vivid, if foolhardy, aspiration. They jostle and drift, passing through each other, less ghosts than the remains of ghosts dressed in shreds of antebellum glory. Half-bodied ladies in evening wear mingle and merge in pale, penetrating intimacy with eyeless gentlemen and soldiers with missing limbs that are not the result of battle. An unseemly dance of post-mortal transparencies. And there are actual dancers among them. An elderly couple, an unfinished sketch with traces of life—a rouge spot, a hint of melanin—clinging to their no-colored gauzy faces, faces that in their decrepitude have a rotted look, like lepers with ragged eyeholes and vacancies for mouths… they flicker into view and whirl, courtly, rickety, gliding away into the ghostly throng, becoming indistinguishable, elements of a gentle, insubstantial chaos, a tattered lace of being.

Captivated, growing accustomed to the cold, Sanie watches them come and go. They intersect each other's paths, yet they seem to apprehend her presence and avoid touching her as she moves along the hall toward the stairs. She has no doubt they're real, not hallucinations, except in the sense that everything is hallucination. The Bullard stamp is on their features, that soft bewildered fleshiness that on occasion veers into a sharper beauty, as with Jackson. This is how he spent his childhood, then. Walking with ghosts, his soul shaped by their ineffable touches. No wonder, she thinks. No wonder.

In among the frail revenants are more substantial figures, and there appears at first to be some correspondence between their modern dress and style and their solidity, making it appear that these relics have degraded over time; but the sight of several Confederate-era spirits without any missing parts persuades her that, while this might be the general rule, some factor in addition to time must be involved. The stairwell, too, is occupied and the second floor. She pauses on the landing for a peek along the hall, but does not go sightseeing. Some of the phantoms at the far end look as tissuey and improbable as the deep-sea jellyfish and tubeworms she's seen on the Discovery Channel.

She doesn't want Jackson to see her in this state (You mean, South Carolina? Heh, heh), but she wants to see him and thinks if she's quiet, he won't notice her spying. She needs to reassure herself about him, though she's not sure what form of assurance she needs. She hovers beside the study door. The room radiates chilliness like an open freezer. She cranes her neck, takes a look. Jackson's at the desk, poring over a book, his pencil poised above a legal pad. Behind him, facing a bookcase, stands a naked old man with withered flanks and unkempt gray hair falling to his shoulders. If it were not for a slight dullness of coloration, his pasty skin a shade too pallid, she might presume him to be alive. His profile and Jackson's are nearly the same, as are their attitudes: entranced, fixed, unswerving. It's apparent they're father and son. Rayfield's head twitches toward her. He's aware of her, at least it seems he is. He stares, his expression grows fretful.

...Sanie, can you see me? I wish you...

Stronger than ever before, yet still softspoken, the voice draws her away from the door.

...If you can't see me, I don't know what I'll do...

The grayed wallpaper billows like old sails decorated with fleurs-de-lis. The floor is a rippling woodgrain river, and the door glows faintly yellow, blurred, but the chest-high pad of rubberized stuff on its unhinged edge, where you're supposed to push so the oils of your skin won't stain the finish, it's dead black, perfectly in focus—it looks as if a light is shining through the wood, yet can't penetrate the pad.

…Sanie… you have to look close if you want to see me…

A weathered, frizzy-haired, middle-aged man and a younger guy with a mustache materialize up ahead. *Poof,* they just pop out of nowhere. They're facing one another, their mouths are working, but she can't hear a thing. Real as a silent film. They both are dressed in jeans and a pin-striped uniform shirt—like those worn by delivery men—with script names embroidered on the pockets. Ralph and Sonny.

…You don't take a chance, you'll never see anything…

She edges between the men and they wink out, as if they were a ghostly union and she's severed their connection. It unsettles her to think they're substantial enough for her to have an affect on them, but she keeps walking and puts a hand on the kitchen door, on the pad.

…Hear what I'm telling you, Sanie? Look close, look deep. One glimpse is all you need…

This articulation, more complex than any previous, unsettles her further. She thinks maybe she should leave the door unopened, but before she can give the idea due consideration, a burst of what-the-hell overrides caution and she pushes into the kitchen.

His back to her, a well-muscled man with longish brown hair, naked from the waist up, is squatting beside the back door, partially blocking Sanie's view of a woman, who appears to have fallen. The man's skin gleams under the overhead light. Strands of hair are stuck to the sweat on his shoulders. He's blocking her view of the woman's face; she has on a pair of cut-offs. Squares of linoleum show scars and ridges, everything's ultra-real, except there's no depth to the scene and, unlike the remainder of the room, the figures don't billow and haven't acquired auras.

…Sanie…

And that's it. What she's been led to see lasts about a second. The man and the woman are gone, their images switched off, and Sanie's equal parts perplexed and freaked out. If that was her on the floor, and she believes it might have been, and if the man was Frank Dean, and she's half-persuaded it was because of his stature, his hair… if that's true, she doesn't understand anything. She's not a ghost, Frank Dean's not a ghost. The peyote's the only explanation. She's tripping, hallucinating. Yet Will hears the voice, too, though—as has been observed—he's not the most reliable witness and it's obvious that he hasn't been forthcoming with her.

Trying to understand, it's like ramming her head into a wall. She needs to get out of there, to loosen the knot the problem has tied in her brain, so she heads for the rear door and steps into the back yard. It's as if she has emerged from a cave after years underground. The sun collects her, owns her. Buzzing, sighing heat and rippling weeds. The intricacy of nature, its shapes and colors newly particularized, washes over her. She feels simplified, absorbed into a unity. She wanders away from the house, revolted by its confining deadness now that she's been exposed to the natural world, and finds a piece of ground where she can sit and be hidden from out-the-window-looking eyes among weeds and broken cornstalks. After sitting a while, she lies down. Things come to her. Oddly configured insights. She wants to remember them, but there's too much to remember. She gives up and watches ants crawling over her arms and legs. The husk of a cricket lies beneath old silver-gray threads of cornsilk, its brittleness and delicacy the answer to a Mandarin riddle. A mummified ear of feed corn once was a glowing hive city. Slender green people peer from among the stalks. Androgynous corn spirits with sly uncomplicated faces. The day slides past, controlling her mood with light and shade. In early afternoon she sneaks back into the house, retrieves a bottle of water and two pears, and hurries back to her spot, oppressed by the humming refrigerator, the electricity in the walls. The pears taste like the essential pears. She's so hungry she eats the cores. She imagines that she can see the translucent currents of wind circling the house.

Near dusk, straightening out a little, she has an insight. Ghosts, according to Will's magazines, are sad fractions left over from the past—that's the consensus according to Will's magazines. But maybe they're actually shadows cast forward in time. And maybe they cast shadows backward in time as well, and some are shadows cast by events that haven't yet happened, or have already happened in some other dimension. This could be the beginning of a larger theory, or, and she tends to go with this choice, she may be overly influenced by Will's magazines and have a screw loose. Her mind is tired from being stretched. She's starting to get shaky and the reek of drying peyote sweat is hard to bear. Wobbling to her feet, she glimpses Frank Dean's black panel van beetling along the dirt road. Ugly and shiny, like a carapace of chitin. It slows passing the house, then picks up speed and vanishes in a wake of dust toward Snade's Corners. The sight forces her to acknowledge that a problem may exist. But at the moment she wants, sustenance, a hot shower, clean clothes. All else must wait. The kitchen lights are on. Rectangular yellow eyes with crosshair pupils. Jackson walks in front of one. The prospect of having to stand for inspection and answer questions is daunting. Where've you been? How'd you get so dirty? What are you looking at? Yet like a convict wise to the ways of prison, she knows how to manipulate the system.

NINE

In the bathroom Sanie goes to staring open-mouthed at the beautiful silver water pouring from the shower head and half-drowns herself. She's still too stoned to deal with the outside world, but the situation demands that she deal with it. If she saw what she thought she saw in the kitchen, if she interpreted it correctly (big ifs), it might be beneficial to get a clearer read on Frank Dean. Looking at him through the lens of the drug may allow her to pick up something she missed. Once she's dry, she puts on an ankle-length skirt and a camp shirt, husband-pleasing clothes, and heads downstairs to find Jackson. He's lingering over an open book and an empty dinner plate in the kitchen. After a cursory glance at her, he refits his eyes to the book.

"Going somewhere?" he asks.

"The Boogie Shack."

He repeats the name as if it were a question, giving it a scornful presentation.

"Frank Dean's band's playing. I thought I'd catch a set. You seen the car keys?"

Jackson's mouth firms. "Are you serious?"

"Yup. Car keys?"

Usually a disapproving "are-you-serious" is enough to make her back down. Jackson can't seem to muster a response.

"It's no big thing," she says. "I'll only be gone an hour or so."

He shakes his head as if what she's proposing is beyond his comprehension. "I can't let you go to a place like that by yourself."

"A place like what? Have you been there?"

"I don't have to be prescient to know that a bar named the Boogie Shack isn't the Russian Tea Room."

She has the urge to tell him the Russian Tea Room's not what she wants, and, to her surprise, her inhibitions shredded by the drug, she blurts it out, saying she needs to be somewhere people are having normal stupid wrong-headed immoral fun and the Boogie Shack sounds about right.

"Fine." He closes the book with a peremptory thump.

"What're you doing?"

"Going with you. What did you expect?"

"I expect you to tell me where the keys are."

When he puts his petulance on full display, as he does now, she almost always caves; but this time, because she doesn't trust her motor skills, because it accords with her plans, she bears his displeasure, and she's glad, once they're on the road, that she didn't insist on driving. Speed is a continuum that rattles her, rekindling her high. The SUV is unwieldy, lurching over the ruts, and the landscapes that bloom in the headlights are darkly bizarre. Her eyes snap from one malformed shape to another. Trees and shrubs and fences are puzzles she has to unsnarl before she can recognize them. Their momentum frightens her and she braces against the dash. Jackson's not speaking to her, and she's grateful for that. Along with everything else, she doesn't believe she could handle a conversation.

A couple of dozen cars and pick-ups are parked in the

gravel lot outside the Boogie Shack, their hoods nosed up to gray concrete block walls, gleaming under the electric bulbs mounted under the eaves. The neon sign atop the roof spells out the name of the place in red-white-and-blue letters, lighting one letter at a time, then blinking them all on and off, a patriotic display that captivates Sanie. Inside, air-conditioned coolness and the beery smell of redneck frenzy. The thumping din she heard from without clarifies into country rock. Arm-waving torsos sprout like furniture-outlet centaurs from tables ringing the dance floor. Dancers painted by revolving red and purple lights strobe in and out of view. Situated on a knee-high stage, the band, lit by steadier red and purple, seems marginally more material. There's too much noise, too much glare, too much everything, and Sanie is disoriented, but after a minute or two, beer in hand, she settles in. Beside her, Jackson, annoyed by the fact that the bar doesn't carry his brand of gin, glumly makes do with a well-liquor martini. One bartender, a busty thirtyish woman in a tank top, her left arm sleeved in a complicated tattoo of tigers and sinister half-faces peeking out of jungle foliage, takes a special interest in Sanie. She pats her hand, calls her "honey," manages a brief shouted conversation, asking where she's from, does she live around here, obviously flirting, and Sanie, thoughts racing, mentally experiences an alternate universe in which she goes home with the bartender, initiates a passionate relationship that, after years of intimacy and companionable talk, dissolves into rancor when Sanie remembers that she's not into women. She laughs at the hyperkinetic pace of the fantasy—like fast-forwarding a video—and Jackson asks, "What's so funny?"

She shakes her head, points to an ear and mouths, Nothing.

The bass player's too short to be Frank Dean, which means FD is the drummer, a shadow with violet shines in his hair, hunched over his kit. He's crisp and professional. She can tell he's bored by how he throws in an occasional jazz fill that doesn't belong, a snide comment on the band's rootsy groove. Ryan, the bearded singer, he's not bad, though his rock star posturing comes off silly in an armpit like the Boogie Shack and the song he's singing is too tall for his range. Sanie likes the music, though. It's the same music she danced to in high school, in Carrboro bars she charmed her way into, using a fake ID that said she was twenty-two. She wouldn't mind dancing now. But Jackson's staring grimly at a neon beer ad, as if he's seen his ancient enemy. So much for dancing. She wonders why they can't admit their mutual mistake. She thinks there has to be a deeper reason than the ones she knows—control issues, childishness—because they apply only to him. What's wrong with *her*? What makes her cling to him?

"You're an enabler," Brittany told her. "You didn't know what you were buying into, but now you enable him to abuse you verbally, to control you, so naturally he does."

Is that all?

She thinks she must be guilty of more than that. If she asked for Jackson's opinion on the subject, he would list her every fault, flaws he once celebrated as virtues. Making it sound as if he's saying something flattering, he'll infer that he loves her in spite of the items on his list. She's like a defective puppy he had as a boy, one he loved fussing over.

"If it was me," Brittany said, "I'd leave him in a flash. Why you stay, why you let him treat you like that… It's degrading."

The song ends and receives a spatter of applause, a few gleeful whoops. Unstrapping his guitar, the lead leans to the singer's mike and says sullenly, "Thanks for the clap."

"We're Local Prophet, Junior!" the singer announces. "You can catch us every weekend here at the…" Someone cuts the sound on the PA and he gives the mike a slap as if it were the culprit.

On break, the band members go in separate directions, mingling with people at different tables. The juke box plays louder than the band did. Frank Dean's talking with a bouncer by the door when he notices Sanie. He waves, signs off on his conversation, and heads over. Halfway to Sanie, he picks up on Jackson, sees they're connected. It shows in a miniscule devaluation of his smile, but his step doesn't falter.

"How y'all doing?" he says, and sticks out his hand to Jackson. "Frank Dean." He's wearing a green Hawaiian shirt with a design of bears driving jitneys.

Jackson gives him a grudging shake and says, "I know who you are," and Sanie tries to cover his rudeness by saying, "This is Jackson."

Frank Dean displays a joint that's been tucked behind his ear. "I'm gonna burn this outside. Y'all wanna join me?"

Before Jackson can speak, Sanie hops down from the barstool and says, "Sure."

Outside, around the corner from the entrance, leaning against a black Camaro with a Confederate flag painted on its roof, Sanie looks up into the starless sky. A tension she didn't realize was there drains from her. It seems that all enclosures, no matter how consoling, be they bars, houses, marriages, breed a poisonous tension. She wants to write down what she sees and feels, not because it's profound, but because she's registering the sensory world with such forceful precision. Heart muscling along, breasts hefted in silk, cunt in neutral, sex drive idling. The breathless night simmering with crickets; the hoods of the cars glistening like hard candy. Heat like an oven left on Warm. The gravel at her feet appears to be shifting, the way popcorn does when a few kernels start to pop. She's still stoned out of her mind, not immersed in hallucination, but capable of revisiting that state effortlessly.

Beside her, taking a stab at being companionable, Jackson says, "Fueling up for the next set?"

"Naw, I'm done. We only do two sets on Sunday." Frank Dean flicks his lighter, his cheeks hollow as he draws in smoke. He offers the joint to Jackson, exhales.

"Pass." Jackson gives a backhanded wave.

"You the designated driver, are ya?"

Jackson mutters, "The designated something."

Sanie sips at the joint, uncertain if she'll like it. The smoke reminds her of the weeds she lived in that afternoon. Ordinary and bitter green. Her head balloons; her thoughts glide higher, spacier.

"Good shit, huh?" Jackson says.

Frank Dean apparently doesn't notice that he's being sarcastic. "Not bad for homegrown. I got a'hold of some Thai seeds. They grew up right fair."

"So you're a connoiseur." Jackson makes the word sound nastily French.

"Don't know 'bout that," says Frank Dean, coolly.

Sanie remembers her mission. "So tell us about LA. Did you work with any big stars?"

Frank Dean's eyes linger on Jackson, then he says, "I did a couple of tours with Chrissie Hynde when her drummer died."

"Really?"

"Yeah… and I did some studio stuff with Warren Zevon and Lionel Ritchie. Tina Turner. Whole buncha folks." Frank Dean hits the joint again and lets out smoke when he speaks. "Biggest star I worked with, I guess, was Jack Nicholson. He rented out a studio just for him and some pals to mess around in. They needed a drummer and I got the call."

"So what was he like?"

Frank Dean shrugs. "Kinda guy probably was the class clown back in high school. 'Course I don't know how much of that was him playing Jack. Most every actor I've met plays themselves when they're out in public."

"Maybe you should have done an analysis," Jackson says.

"How do you mean?" asks Frank Dean.

"You know. Seized the opportunity to sort out the private man from the public. So you could answer questions like this. I mean, if you tell the story often—as I imagine you do—the question's bound to crop up."

Frank Dean seems to choose his words carefully. "That never occurred to me," he says, taking the joint from Sanie. He squints at Jackson as he inhales.

"You want to *use* a story like that," Jackson says. "Work it up into material. Embellish it a little. How you went out drinking with Jack and the guys afterward. How the two of you bonded and all."

"Now why'd I want to do that?"

There it is! The tone struck by the voice in the house, though the timbre's off. Soft and enticing… except with Frank Dean, the tone isn't enticing in the usual sense, it's menacing, like he's telling Jackson, Keep on with that shit and see what you get. The ghost voice might be angry in that same way.

"It's a fantastic icebreaker," says Jackson. "I can't tell you how many times I've been in a situation when I wished I could say, 'That puts me in mind of the time I played drums with Jack Nicholson.'"

"You frequently find yourself in difficult situations, do you?"

"Yes. Of course I do. It comes with challenging oneself, with trying to achieve something in life." Jackson makes a loose gesture that seems to include Frank Dean. "Rather than the opposite."

Frank Dean settles against the fender of the car parked next to the Camaro. "Tell you the truth, me and Jack did do some hanging out."

Jackson shoots Sanie a glad, bug-eyed look, as if to say, Isn't that astonishing?

"Yeah, we went out that night and many other nights," Frank Dean goes on. "We got to be tight. We'd talk for hours sometimes. And each time we'd begin our conversation with the same topic. We'd tell each other about the biggest pussy we'd run into since last we'd met. That was *our* little icebreaker." He hits the joint lightly and offers it to Sanie, who declines. "Many's the night since I left LA, I've wished he was here."

Jackson's having a hard time keeping his smile straight and Sanie wishes now that she had risked driving alone. "I could use another beer," she says. "Let's go on back in."

"Some nights," Frank Dean continues. "Like tonight, for instance. I almost feel like Jack's here in spirit. Like we're sitting over a couple of whiskeys and I'm getting set to tell him my latest pussy-of-the-week experience."

"I'm going in!" Sanie grabs Jackson's elbow, moves him with her shoulder.

Frank Dean flicks the fire off the tip of the joint, drops the roach into his pocket. He says something as they walk away, but Sanie's too angry to hear it. Angry at Jackson because he lives to put down anyone she brings into their circle—the only people he deems worthy of associating with are those he knows or, to a lesser degree, those whom they know together. Angry at Frank Dean because she assumes he's worldly enough to recognize Jackson's arrogance for a pose. Mainly she's angry at herself for bringing the two men together. No matter how she spins it, she knows on some level it was a high school play.

She drinks a beer at the bar, Jackson sulking beside her, then goes out into the parking lot while he settles the bill. She's trying to recall where they parked, when a woman's voice calls, "G'night, now!" The blond bartender is leaning beside the door, one knee drawn up, her foot braced on the wall, smoking a cigarette. Standing beneath a naked bulb, the smoke pluming into the hot light, the colors of her tattoos glowing—it's a noirish image that brings to mind covers on the old pulp detective magazines Sanie boxed up in her father's study after his death. A tough, lonely redneck moll waiting for Fate, her pockmarked boyfriend. Or girlfriend, in this instance. Sanie waves, and the bartender says, "See ya 'round." They both could be on a cover. Bad girl and good girl eyeing each other on a hot southern nowhere night. Separated by a river of gravel and a world of experience. What will they do and which is which? That would be the subject of the story inside.

Jackson steps through the door, spots Sanie, glances to his left to see what she's looking at. He jerks his eyes away from the bartender as if they've touched something vile and beelines for the car without a word to Sanie. He knows that she'll follow, and she supposes she will. She doesn't believe that she can pull off becoming a lesbian, though certain aspects of it would be easier than the ride home's going to be.

TEN

Here's how it works between them. It's up to Sanie to apologize whenever something happens that displeases Jackson, even if she's not to blame. If she withholds apology, he withdraws from her, limiting their contact to brisk, superficially cheerful interactions. It's like he's telling her if he can't have the relationship on his terms, he won't have it at all. Every situation, it's the same. If he doesn't agree with her choice of dinner guests, videos, vacation destinations, he'll have no dinner, no video, no vacation rather than agree. He'll do without, he'll suffer for his beliefs. He'll lock himself inside himself and refuse to have fun again. Of course he never agrees. There's not a single subject, be it ever so trivial, that he won't argue. Her taste, her moral compass, her intellectual convictions—they're all flawed, misguided, uninformed. The worthlessness of her judgments is the foundation of his good moods.

Ordinarily, isolated with him, bound by habit and convention, she's too busy doing chores, running errands, proofing his papers, and the rest to have much time either for friends or for herself—without him to talk to, the sensory deprivation gets to her and she gives in quickly. But at the Bullard house, though she's essentially alone, his withdrawal doesn't feel like deprivation and she can't understand this, quite. A few days ago she was climbing

70

the walls, a "bored-shitless wife." Yet now that she's withheld apology for a record-setting thirty-six hours, she's... What's the word? Happy? Happyish, at any rate. Energized. Hopeful. It's as if she, too, has an elastic band attached and it's about to snap. She hasn't made a conscious decision to leave Jackson, but this unexpected feeling of liberation suggests to her that the vote may be in.

The first night of non-apology, she's too nervous to enjoy it. She's violating a taboo and dreads repercussions. She tells herself that she should apologize—after all, the unpleasantness at the Boogie Shack was, seminally, her fault. But she's apologized so many times for forgetting something at the store, for inviting someone over who hasn't passed inspection, for hating a movie filled with exploding heads, she figures he owes her. The next morning, walking into the sunlit kitchen, she's decided it's not worth the hassle and intends to apologize, but seeing him at the table with his law book and cereal, poised to be forgiving, expecting her to cave in, that's the moment her elastic band snaps... or at least loses much of its elasticity. As she pours coffee and hunts up a box of breakfast bars, his eyes track her, waiting, waiting, and when she turns, leans against the sink, cup in hand, and says, "'Morning," he closes his book and sits back in the chair, his head tipped to the side, face neutral, like a priest prepared to hear confession, calm and accepting, readying a penance. This pisses her off so much, her hand trembles as she sips her coffee. Apology won't come. The bargain that's been struck between them, her self-esteem in return for his tranquility, no longer seems a bargain. The reward he bestows—trifling conversation, a few minutes of pleasantness, an absolving kiss—no longer seems a reward. She stuffs a breakfast bar into the hip pocket of her cut-offs.

"See you later," she says.

She spends the morning on the porch steps, making lists in a stenographer's notebook she bought at Snade's. In the past her lists have been wishes, like the lists she wrote as a child. Get Masters degree, register with temp agency, and look into cheap housing are no more realistic to her mind than become rock star, marry screen idol, live in Tangiers. But though this morning's lists are similarly constructed, they seem to be comprised of possibilities, not fantasies. It startles her to recognize that she may have a future, one that's not merely an adjunct to Jackson's, an endless repetition of the present, and yet it's exhilarating, too. Leaving is less frightening a prospect than staying. She believes she's reached that point. Almost, anyway.

The sun drugs her, lulling her to torpor. She's got a funny sort of hangover from the peyote—head thick, joints achy—and it would be easy to sleep. Fat bugs buzz past like stray rounds. Frank Dean's van rolls by without slowing, but—to her surprise—he waves. That starts her thinking about the previous night. The mission. Hearing him speak with the ghost's voice (nearly the ghost's voice, at any rate), its unhurried inflections. She wonders if she can trust her memory. If so, is the similarity between the two voices more than a coincidence? Though she recalls why she went to the Boogie Shack, she's too lethargic to penetrate the air of unreality that now attaches to her formless suspicions. Maybe, she tells herself, she was only searching for a spark to kick over her engine.

Will's off somewhere, probably hanging out at the Piggly Wiggly, watching Allie dispense sticky buns and éclairs, and that afternoon, following a nap, Sanie goes poking around his room, looking for a video. She discovers that what she presumed was a closet door leads to a small windowless sitting room lined with bookshelves, furnished with two unspeakably ugly armchairs upholstered in a shiny olive-and-red striped material, a little cherrywood table standing between them, a hooked rug like a many-colored puddle on the floor. Most of the books are novels. Faulkner, Walker Percy, Hammett; a variety of more recent, less distinguished works, heavy on Grisham and King. There's also a smattering of southern history, a series of do-it-yourself manuals, and, stuck at the end of one shelf, four composition books with the name Rayfield Bullard in neat handwriting on the covers. Sanie curls up in one of the chairs and begins leafing through them.

The books contain page after page of cramped script detailing the growth of the Bullard family tree, material of no greater interest to Sanie than those interminable daisy chains of "begats" found in the Bible. The first of them records Bullard history into the mid-seventeenth century, when Henry Bullard, wounded during the Seven Years' War, sailed with his wife Nora to America, and there took possession of a land grant awarded for his courageous service. The second and third are devoted to the spread of the family in the United States. Basically more of the same, but with one distinction. In the margins next to some of the names are scribbled dates spanning a period between 1987 and 1996, the year Rayfield died. Certain names are annotated with multiple dates, and some of the dates end with question marks. Madeleine Bullard (1854–1882), the great-great-granddaughter of Henry and Mary, has fourteen such dates crammed together beside her name and three of them—November 29, 1989; July 12, 1992; October 26, 1993—have question marks appended.

Sanie's puzzling over these marginalia when she hears Jackson calling to her. His voice holds a questioning tone and by this she knows he's dipped deeper into the handbook of marital tactics. He'll act the penitent, draw her into a superficial discussion of their problems and, in the process, his penitence will morph into tender concern. Does she feel all right? Is she having migraines again? Thus implying that her fit of stubbornness is a result of a physical problem, some female thing for which she's not responsible. It's an out he offers her. He'll inundate her with false sympathy—though he won't perceive it as false—until, weary of it all, she apologizes for the accident of gender. She gets to her feet, tiptoes to the door of the sitting room, shuts and locks it.

She remains on edge even after he stops calling. Unable to concentrate, she sets the book aside and dozes in the chair. Noises from the next room wake her. Muddled, she can't unscramble them, but as her head clears she understands that Will and Allie are making love. Throbbing monkey love, by the sound. Sanie would never have expected it, but Will's a talker. He gives instructions, offers profane endearments and compliments, dialogue straight out of an old porno flick. Allie responds with spacey cooings. It's as if Goldilocks and Papa Bear are having a fling in the woodland cottage. Sanie can't imagine the levels of fantasy necessary to transform Will into this bedroom Godzilla. Fifteen minutes go by. Twenty-five minutes. She grows wistful, remembering the last time she fucked for that long. With a geology grad student, her freshman year at Carolina, six months before she met Jackson. Thinking about it gets her aroused. After thirty-five minutes she wonders, What if they're at it all night? But at the forty-two-minute mark, Allie yields up a broken, swooning cry and Will disgorges a mighty grunt. She can hear them talking afterward, moving around the room, boards creaking under their feet. And then silence. It's like a little fire has gone out, and Sanie, still aroused, unbuttons her cut-offs, just the top button, and slips her right hand down into her panties. She's wetter than she realized, and when she touches her clit, a warm wave lifts through her body and for a second she worries someone will hear, that Jackson will pound on the door, but she doesn't want to stop and soon the cut-offs and panties are around her ankles and she slips a finger inside herself to collect her oils, bringing them forth to rub onto her clit, rubbing feverishly, and she needs him inside, she aches for him, the "he" that sometimes has a face, sometimes not, but he isn't ever there enough, he's not enough there, so she imagines his cock, she licks it and takes the head in her mouth, and it's hard, thick, hot, yet almost weightless on her tongue, like it's made of balsa wood, and she wants him to come on her breasts, to massage his sperm into her nipples, and it gets all crazy and disjointed, images, urges, her hips thrashing, and before long she's biting the name of Jesus in half to stop from shouting it, and digging her fingers into the arm of the chair, belly heaving, legs splayed and stiff until the finishes, and then she presses her thighs together, keeping her right hand in place, and draws up her knees, trying to hold onto the heat, the involvement, the feeling that's ebbing from her. She's shocked by the intensity of her orgasm, by how quickly it happened. Usually it takes her a while.

She dresses hurriedly, her haste fueled by guilt over this imaginary, impersonal infidelity, and by the cold. These plantation houses were built to keep things cool, and sometimes, even in the summer, they can be uncomfortably so. And, too, she has the feeling that she's being watched. She's grown accustomed to constant oversight from living with Jackson, but this has engaged her spider senses, set the back of her neck to prickling, and she'd swear that a mysterious figure is standing behind the bookshelves, peering through a hollowed-out edition of *The Firm* or *Christine*. Louise, perhaps. Wearing a monk's robe over a bustier. Sanie can't quite laugh it off. All buttoned and tucked, she unlocks the door and peeks out. Will's room is empty. As she crosses the room, she catches sight of several *objets d'amour* on the floor beside the bed. A large vibrator, a finger-sized pink vibrator covered in wartlike bumps, tubes of flavored lubricants, discarded packaging bearing the name The Anal Intruder, and, still in its unopened box, half-obscured behind a sun-glazed plasticene panel, something green and pointy and menacing. She kneels and takes a peek. It's a toy figurine, an alien monster with tentacles and a fearsome visage and even more fearsome potential than the Anal Intruder. Curiously enough, it seems not at all out of place, standing shoulder-to-shoulder with a little squad of grotesque superheroes arranged in a ragged line, a fresh recruit brought up to reinforce the survivors of a battle.

ELEVEN

Every war should have a name, but Sanie can't come up with one for the war that's been initiated between her and Jackson. The War of Cheerful Grins would be superficially descriptive, as would the War of Scrupulous Politeness. But there's nothing superficial about their conflict. As the days pass, and they're all basically the same day, her acting chipper, Jackson acting unconcerned, brittle smiles and brief, glib exchanges, he in his study, her off running errands or down at Snade's or hiding out in some obscure portion of the house, she realizes that she's fighting for her life. Often when driving into Edenburg, an image of Jackson in denial mode will come before her mind's eye, and she'll bang the heel of her hand on the steering wheel, punch the dash, make some ineffectual gesture of frustration, and say, Jerk! Fucking control freak! Something that serves to encapsulate his essence. Then she firms her lips, drives a little faster, formulates a plan. She'll withdraw half their funds from the bank, head back to Chapel Hill, collect her clothes and possessions, and be off again that same day. She'll spend the night in a Virginia motel and the next day she'll drive straight through to New York, where she can stay with friends, begin a life of substance. No matter what she does, it'll be more substantial than fetching coffee, doing laundry, picking up his dry cleaning, his copies, dropping off his library books, cooking, hosting dinner parties for people he wants to impress... She can't recall at what point during the ten years of the relationship she made the transition from determined young woman to kitchen drudge/gofer/business accessory/sexual appliance, but it's evident that Jackson conditioned her, slowly wore her down with his passive aggression. There will be time later, she thinks, to analyze her imperfections, to assign her portion of blame. For now, while her head's above water and she has a view of the marriage unimpeded by guilt, it's essential that she put some distance between them and get clear of his influence. Yet as always, when she reaches town that day, she does not go to the bank, she does not drive to Virginia or New York, she performs her several wifely duties, checks the mail, picks up Jackson's prescription, does some essential shopping at the Piggly Wiggly, where a person costumed as Mr. Pig (butcher's apron, dress shirt with red stripes, black bow tie, and plastic pig head) is cavorting about the parking lot and attempts to thrust upon her a tray of noxious-looking appetizers; and then, instead of going straight home (as expected) to deliver the mail, medication, and so forth, she engages in a minor act of rebellion and stops in at the town's sole concession to modernity, a coffee shop called The Great Bean, bright and clean and smelling of exotic blends, which occupies a glass storefront on Edenburg's main drag and is run by two sweet souls in their early thirties, Levi and Andy, who dispense designer caffein and pass the time listening to jazz and are, it's said, gay. An affection for jazz is considered one of the seven signs of the homosexual in these parts, the cliché no less odious because, in this case, it's accurate. Levi greets her by name, speaking like he's got a candy mint under his tongue, and, as he makes her latte, says it sure looks like rain.

Sanie takes her double tall mocha to a table by the window and stares mournfully out at the Doodlebug, a sundries shop across the street, a view segmented by ancient parking meters sticking up from curbs so high they have steps, watching a pedestrian passage of farmers, lean, leathery ones with nicotine-stained fingers and baseball caps, and fat ones with sunburned necks, pale as the hogs they butcher, wearing sunglasses and khaki trousers with EZ-Fit elastic waistbands, and matrons towing complaining kids, and teenagers roughhousing as they approach the Tastee Freez, and a wizened old geezer with gray hair, greaser sideburns, and a comb protruding from his back pocket, who glances behind him fitfully as if worried that he's being tailed. A perverted version of Norman Rockwell, Hell on Goober Street, and she's trapped in an air-conditioned bubble inside it. Shame wells up in her, hot and galling. She can't believe how weak-willed she's become. It's useless to blame Jackson; it's her who needs fixing and she hasn't a clue where to begin. She takes out her pen and notebook, hoping writing will help her focus, but she's got too much on her mind and she continues to stare out the window. Levi slips a new disc into the changer and a solo alto sax wails. Ornette Coleman's "Sadness." The first time he played it, she asked him what it was called. She liked it—its soaring, plaintive melody captured her mood. Now he plays it whenever she stops in and she's come to hate it for the very same reason she once liked it. The sky darkens and a scattering of drops freckles the sidewalks. She's been there half an hour and she's written a single word: "rain."

A black man steps out of OC's Pool Room adjoining the Doodlebug, and lights a cigarette. He's followed in short order by Frank Dean, dressed in a green T-shirt and jeans. Sanie perks up. He scans the street, fixes on her SUV, says something to the black man, who laughs; then he jogs across the street as the rain falls harder, heading for the coffee shop. By the time he hits the door, it has increased to a downpour and he enters dripping.

"Hey, there," he says, a little breathless. "I been hoping I'd run into you. Let me get some coffee."

She's still angry over the way he treated Jackson at the Boogie Shack and, as she listens to him putting in his order, joking with Levi, she grows angrier yet because he's so affable, so easy around people, something Jackson has to work at, and she's attracted to that quality, attracted to him, and, with everything else that's going on, she doesn't want to deal with the attraction; in fact, she resents him for it.

"Sorry about the other night," he says. "Your husband caught me off-guard. I don't usually let stuff like that get to me."

Sanie's response is clipped, hostile. "Stuff like what?"

Frank Dean shoots her a quizzical look. "Like the other night at the bar."

"Oh, that." Sanie makes a gesture as if she's flicking crumbs away, and has a sip of her latte.

"I'm not gonna let you stay mad at me," he says after an interval. "Just because your husband and I got to acting like a couple of dogs, that's no reason to get all bent out of shape. Men are prone to act that way around women. He was being territorial and I was an asshole. So how about we put that behind us and talk about, y'know, the weather or something."

His reasonable approach turns down the flame of Sanie's anger a few degrees, yet it gives her another reason to be angry. How dare he be reasonable? She needs anger as a defense.

"Football. You're a southern girl, right? You must be able to talk football. What's up with the 'heels? Is North Carolina going places under Coach Bunting?"

"Oh, yeah. Scary places." She clamps her lips, but it's too late. She pictures her anger dropping like the mercury in a cartoon thermometer, going down so fast it yields a funny sound, a *fwwwp*, and grows an icicle off the bottom.

"I never have understood," he says, "why with all the politically correct bullshit going on, why nobody's ever gone after the name, Tar Heels."

For several minutes, they debate whether or not "tar heel" primarily refers to a person of mixed race or to the fact that North Carolina once commercially produced sizable quantities of pitch; then they debate which is the stronger football conference, ACC or SEC. No longer seeking to forestall the conversation, Sanie tries to prolong it, and she tells him in more detail about the ghost voice, her peyote trip, the strange notations in Rayfield's journals.

"Know who you might want to ask about all this?" Frank Dean grabs her pen and notebook and scribbles on a blank page. "Janine Morrison. She's working now, but you can give her a call and set up a time to talk. She was Rayfield's secretary for a while. She told me about some weird stuff happened to her. I bet she'd be glad to tell you what she knows."

Their conversation loses energy, then, allowing the sexual tension to become more palpable, an actual pull, and Sanie recognizes that they've reached a point where it would be natural to nudge things in a more personal direction, and she has an urge, an almost overwhelming urge, to tell him about the marriage, its lusterless depths and scummy shallows, like a lake whose feeder source is drying up, but she understands that would be prelude to a deeper involvement, making a date to meet again (just coffee, of course), or, and this is not inconceivable to her, going to a motel and smoking up the sheets for an hour or two, until—in a panic—she realizes what she's done. She says nothing to dispel the awkward moment, stares down at her hands, notices she's started chewing her nails again.

"Well…" He peers though the blurred window. "This isn't going to let up anytime soon. I got to get back to the shop." He comes to his feet and smiles at her.

She smiles back and makes a pale joke. "You're dressed so neatly, I thought this must be your day off."

He glances down at his clothes. "I had a meeting at the bank. To discuss my so-called finances. Once I get into old lady Brainard's transmission, I'll soon be restored to my usual grungy state."

He sidles to the door, hangs beside it, and this is the point at which the motel becomes possible. All she has do is to say, "Wait, I'll walk out with you," and stand in the doorway for a second or two, looking up at him, and he'll say hesitantly, "You wanta go somewhere for a while?" and she'll nod, less hesitantly, and that'll be that.

"Okay. I'm gone." He opens the door and, the instant before he runs out into the rain, adds, "Don't get wet, now."

She suspects he may be kicking himself for the subtext of this unnecessary caution, or maybe he half-intended it. One way or the other, it doesn't matter. After just a cup of coffee, it's plain now—if it wasn't already—that they have a lot of subtext.

TWELVE

In the rainy twilight, almost dark as night, the spirits of the house seem to be oppressed, and the corridors, lacking the supernatural luster she's applied to them, have a dead feel, like tunnels burrowed by long-gone termites through the half-rotted wood, and the lamp shades, the wallpaper, every cloth surface, are clammy to the touch, permeated with damp—even the light appears water-damaged and weakened, incapable of reaching into shadowy corners it once illuminated. The study door is shut, a seam of lamp glow beneath it. Relieved at being able to avoid a confrontation, she places Jackson's pills on the floor outside the study and goes upstairs. Voices issue from Will's room. He and Allie are doubtless getting set to play Galactina and the Space Invader—she imagines Will in his boxers, the toy alien in hand, about to apply it to Allie, who pretends to cower. Sanie goes into her room and sits on the edge of the bed. As the walls close in, her mind retreats to the precincts of the no-tell motel toward which she and Frank Dean might have sped, but she stamps out that spark before it catches. Though she's been tempted on several occasions, she's never engaged in an affair, and she's not prepared to do so now, this despite the close call earlier that afternoon. Best not to indulge in fantasies. There must be a reason she's stuck in the marriage, something aside from security and creature comforts and her weakness. A contractual obligation, or some thin loyalty she must satisfy. She needs to comprehend that reason, she thinks, before she can leave. For days, she studies on the problem, but either a solution doesn't exist or else it's beyond her ability to perceive. She does a lot of staring out the kitchen window, analytic thought crumbling into daydreams.

The rain continues, August turning to September, and the gloom in the house begins to feel perpetual, a lunar twilight, damp and chill. She cuts short her trips into town, staying clear of Frank Dean, of all but the most perfunctory interactions; she limits her visits to Snade's Corners, but doesn't cut them out entirely. She needs a place where she can breathe and be herself, where she can kick back and listen to Gar gossip, make a joke and have someone laugh at it, and, though it strikes her as a little odd that she can't find this in the marriage, she's taken refuge in a generalized condemnation of men, a bumper-sticker feminism, and concluded that every marriage has the same level of dysfunction and thus essentially the same character. Otherwise, her conversations are confined to brief chats with Will, who spends much of his time with Allie, and flinty exchanges with Jackson. Their war goes on, but its intensity has diminished. They pretend, as perhaps they have always done, but the pretense of intimacy has fled. She reads. DeLillo, Grisham, Ozick, and, an irony, locked away in her own manor house, the Brontës. Now and again she hears the ghost voice, but she's grown accustomed to it and it no longer has the power to surprise or intrigue—it might as well be a moth batting its wings against a window. She sits long hours in the kitchen, hoping for her muse to alight, notebook and pen at the ready. One afternoon, while she's slumped at the kitchen table, Louise, wearing a flowered housecoat and slippers, bangs in through the door, stops, retreats a step, hovering beside the sink, consternation writ large upon her pudding face. Sanie examines her coolly, then looks down at her notebook, at the words scribbled there, and says, "Do what you need to do. I won't bother you."

Allowing Louise to move about the kitchen, free from scrutiny, forces Sanie to read what she has written and, to her surprise, it's not bad. Too mannered, perhaps, but not bad at all:

"The casement window in Elise Cardozo's bedroom overlooked a section of Prospect Park in Brooklyn, a stretch of walking path framed by maples and ash, and lined with concrete benches, one of which served each morning as the meeting place for a slender young woman—a shopgirl or waitress, judging by her shoes and her flannel jacket—and a middle-aged man with a full salt-and-pepper beard, who dressed rather more expensively. They would arrive (the woman first, usually) shortly after nine o'clock and, without the least preamble, they would begin talking with animated intensity, as if continuing a conversation broken off the day before. Since Elise was in the habit of taking a second cup of coffee sitting at the window, she became a witness to the relationship, such as it was.

"She assumed that the man and woman were lovers going through a difficult patch, but she soon discarded this notion. Though they held hands on occasion, the contact had about it a formal air, and Elise came to think that the man must be an uncle or a cousin who was counseling the woman, ministering to her in some way. Yet the urgency of their speech, the forceful gestures that seemed expressive of anger and dismay, did not support her interpretation.

Nor did the cursory manner in which they tended to part, the man standing, buttoning his overcoat, glancing this way and that as if to reorient himself, then striding off into the park without a backward glance, and the woman, her manner betraying frustration, remaining on the bench a minute or so before moving briskly away in the same direction.

"Elise's curiosity about the pair did not rise to the level of fascination. They posed a trivial puzzle, one she used to clear her mind of the clutter that accrued from breakfast with her husband and chasing her twelve-year-old off to school. Imagining a past for them and scripting their dialogue was just the sort of whimsey that served to rev up her mental apparatus, helping prepare her for a day of more rigorous thought at the computer. She provided them with a detailed family background, with lives hemmed in by dark secrets; she supposed them to be related yet not close, distant cousins—in essence, strangers—driven to complicity in order to combat an evil whose origins were rooted in the intricate history of the blood they shared.

"If there had been more variance in their behavior, she might have sustained her interest, but each successive meeting was identical to the previous one, half an hour of talk leavened by a spot of hand-holding, and after several weeks she became bored, even resentful of the couple's interruption of her view, to see them as an impediment rather than as an aid to clarity, and she might have stopped watching them altogether if she had not unearthed a pair of binoculars while rummaging through a closet, searching for a box of CDs.

"Motivated partly by the hope that she might catch them at some impropriety, something that would give her the leverage necessary to drive them away, she went to the window and trained the binoculars on the bench where the couple was sitting, focusing first upon the man. He was older than she had presumed. Sixtyish. A dark, deeply lined face with a hooked nose, fleshy lips, and hooded eyes. A face that called to mind images of Byzantine royalty. His clothes were stylishly cut, and on his right hand he wore a massive gold ring with a raised design—like a coin made into a ring. When he spoke, he inclined his head and stared intently at the woman, as if trying to beam his message into her brain. Elise had the idea that whatever the exact nature of the message, it was nothing the woman wished to hear.

"The woman listened, downcast, features veiled by the fall of her unfashionably long brown hair; but when she lifted her head, Elise recognized the face as her own. Although the woman was ten or twelve years younger (she appeared to be in her early twenties), in all other aspects, the resemblance was startling. She had Elise's strong cheekbones, her generous mouth, and large hazel eyes. Even the eyebrows were hers, sharply slanted toward the bridge of the nose at what seemed exaggerated angles, and too thick (Elise kept hers plucked). And the nose itself, straight and unremarkable… Elise had always considered it a flaw, but now she saw that it modulated the exotic character of the face's other elements, unifying them, lending sweetness and innocence to what might otherwise have been a seductive mask. She had the urge to run to the bathroom mirror, to determine whether her own face retained these girlish qualities; but she remained at the window, taking in every detail of the woman's appearance. Her jeans and cheap wool coat; her imitation leather bag; her gloveless hands pale and raw from the cold.

"Before Elise could come to terms with the bewilderment

that arose from seeing this apparition of her younger self, the man stood and made his customary abrupt departure; acting on impulse, Elise threw on sweats and tennis shoes, grabbed a coat, and hurried down the stairs, across the street, and out into the park. The woman had left the bench and was already well along the path leading toward 11th Street..."

A writing teacher once told Sanie, when she was distressed by her lack of progress, that writers improve in quantum leaps, that they go along in their daily grind, churning out their usual uninspired stuff, and then suddenly one day they'll spot a glint of gold among the dross, a flicker of the real quill. "Keep at it," the teacher said. "You'll get there." She hadn't believed him, but now... Exhillarated, she reads the passage again, making minor changes that reduce the Victorian flavor. The biggest leap of all, she thinks, is that she knows where the story's going. Sort of, anyway. The distance in the house, the tiny space she's carved out in the marriage by virtue of the war with Jackson, it's permitted her to think more clearly. The sound of chair legs scraping startles her and she looks up to see that Louise has taken the seat across from her. Sanie's curiosity overrides her aggravation at being interrupted, and she waits for her sister-in-law to speak.

Louise's helmet hair lends her squarish, jowly face an unfortunate masculinity; her hands, clasped beneath her breasts, wrestle with one another, the fingers flexing as if trying to gain an advantage. The floral pattern on her housecoat is, Sanie estimates, about twenty percent old foodstains. Seconds lag past and finally Sanie says, "Hey."

Louise says, "Hey," back, but it seems a reflex response, a fearful one, a yip.

Baffled, Sanie asks if Louise found what she was after, thinking this may be the problem—she's forgotten where the spoons are kept, where the oatmeal cookies are shelved.

Louise stretches out her hand, trembling a little, and rests it atop Sanie's. "I used to be like you," she says, and nods vigorously as if to assure Sanie of this improbability.

"Used to be?" Sanie chooses her words carefully, not wanting to spook her. "You're like me now."

"No."

Announced in a half-whisper, with a tremor that hinges it in the middle, it's the saddest "no" Sanie has ever heard, seeming to embody a world of miserable experience.

"It happened here." Louise casts her eyes up to the ceiling, darts them about, reminding Sanie of a cat tracking an airborne mite.

"In the kitchen?" Sanie hasn't a clue as to what Louise is going on about, but figures it will be easier to pin down location before trying to clarify the nature of the event.

Louise nods. "Everywhere, but here first."

At a loss, Sanie gives up on location and asks, "Does this have anything to do with the ghosts?"

Louise's eyes widen. "You see them?"

"I did once."

"They're not ghosts. 'Least not all of them."

Jackson bursts into the room so forcefully that the door smacks against the wall, and Louise snatches her hand from Sanie's grasp. An imperious glare, contrived for Sanie's benefit, lapses when Jackson notices his sister. He pauses, allows himself a smirk, and says, "Ladies." Then he opens the refrigerator and begins to rummage inside it. "We don't have any cheese?"

"You should know, you're the only one eats it," says Sanie.

"The youngest have it the worst," Louise whispers, a comment that Sanie relegates to the realm of daft utterance; she's been put on edge by Jackson's unexpected appearance.

"Pick some up, will you." Jackson closes the refrigerator door; he's holding a carrot stick. "And some of those stone wheat crackers. Get enough to last." He rolls his shoulders, working out the kinks. "So what are you up to?" After an interval during which no one speaks, he says snidely, "That question was for the entire panel."

Louise looks up pertly and Sanie says, "Talking."

"Talking, huh?" Jackson has a bite of carrot. "What about? Cold temperature physics? Economic infrastructure in the Horn of Africa?"

Both women stare at him, Louise in bewilderment, Sanie with veiled contempt.

"Sharing recipes, perhaps?" Jackson leans on the refrigerator, bemused, munching his carrot.

"I've got a recipe for blackberry pie that Daddy said could save the planet," says Louise.

This reference to his father appears to unsettle Jackson, but he covers it up and says, "You'll have to fix it for supper sometime. We could do with a little saving around here."

"Blackberries aren't in season," says Louise mournfully.

"Any sort of home-cooking would be nice." Jackson looks pointedly at Sanie. "Maybe you can make us some of your spoonbread."

"I don't think… I've got all the fixin's. But… I…"

Louise falters and Jackson says, "Sanie'll pick up whatever you need. Just give her a list. Why don't you go write one up?"

"A list. I…" All the solidity, the energy that funded Louise's coherence, is broken by Jackson's demand. She stands, raises a hand in a partially completed gesture, and says to Sanie, "I'm going now."

She continues to hover beside the table, her mouth working silently.

"Off you go, sis! Down the rabbit hole." Jackson gives her a delicate push, like he's setting a toy boat adrift. As Louise scurries for the door, he steps close behind, steering her with his palm and says to Sanie, "Pick up some corn muffins, too."

After he's gone, Sanie sits fuming. Jerk. Asshole. Bastard. Once she calms down, she wonders if Jackson intended to disrupt the conversation she was having with Louise. When they first arrived, he encouraged her to get to know his siblings. Then she realizes that such a turnaround is in keeping with his pattern of behavior. He wants what she wants until she begins to achieve it. Like with her writing. She used to show him things from time to time, and it was always, "I really like what you're doing here," blah blah blah, but since she's sold a few pieces, though he has been effusive in his praise, there's a subtle restraint in his voice, an undertone of indifference, inquiries as to how much she was paid (not much), all of which acts to reduce the effect of his praise to a pat on the head that keeps her tail wagging, but causes her to question the worth of what she's done. She tries to put her head back together by re-reading the passage she wrote that morning, but on this pass it strikes her as overwrought and juvenile. Obviously, it's a wish-fulfillment story, number three on Professor

Demery's list of Things-A-Novice-Writer-Should-Avoid. Her protagonist is a stand-in for her. Removed from life, having to view it from a window or through binoculars. Escaping her cloistered existence by running after her younger self. *Gah!* It's sappy, crappy, unhappy housewife stuff. Sanie sees no way to make it anything other than what it is, but she doesn't crumple it up and throw it away. Obeying Demery's Fourth Dictum (Save Everything), she turns the page. She's tempted to blame Jackson for souring her on what she thought was competent, but she can't make him the fall guy for every failure—though his shadow darkens everything she undertakes, she has to outface that reality. She understands that her success is ultimately up to her and, with this conviction in mind, she addresses pen to paper.

There's a character she's been thinking of attempting, a woman, not her at another age, not a shell that embodies her wishes, her desires, but a woman she knew when she was a girl growing up in Asheville, before her family moved to Chapel Hill. A spinster in her fifties, a doctor who would travel up into the hills to treat the backwoods people, the snake worshippers, the rickety fiddlers and dobro players, the untutored and the unwashed, the natural, native survivalists who did not survive into the new millennium... A woman about whose habituations and appetites implausible tales were told, tales that posed a contradiction to her outward manner, which was decorous, gentle, attentive to whoever was speaking with her. The tales may not have been true, but the woman knew about them and never sought to deny them, perhaps because she couldn't be bothered with what people said about her. Sanie, age eleven, asked her if one story, especially scurrilous, were true, and the woman, she was called

Melora by everyone, said, "Honey, don't you believe if I did all those things you heard about, I did 'em the right way?" At that moment, for no reason Sanie could fathom, Melora seemed powerful and, though ancient, incredibly beautiful. For several years she was something of an icon for Sanie, until Sanie discovered that boys liked her, albeit mostly not the right boys, not the boys she liked, and all the derangement and obsession and terror that passes for high school set her a'spin. Now she's inclined to take a more clinical view of Melora. She wants to believe all the stories and to imagine the interior life of a woman capable of consorting with hillbilly devils and murderers, at once violent and tender, nurturing and dangerous, deviant and high-principled, laboring like a saint and sexually voracious. It's the way she assumes many women would be if they didn't have the soul squeezed out of them by new age diets and religion and more sophisticated targeted marketing schemes. Sanie sometimes thinks that she's like Melora—she has, after all, a similar sensibility. But then she'll catch sight of herself in the special mirror Jackson's fabricated for her and that notion goes glimmering. She concentrates, trying to capture Leilah with a few deft strokes of the pen, but it's tough-going. After a while, she looks out the window. Bird mess streaks the glass. It's still raining.

THIRTEEN

…Sanie…

"Go away! Shoo!"

Sanie… won't you look at…

"Shush!"

Sanie… Sanie…

"You know what? Shut up!"

I wish…

"So what would happen, huh? If I could see you. What's the big deal?"

Sanie…

"You think I'd throw myself at you? You probably look like crap, being dead and all."

It's been so long…

"Yeah, my heart aches so bad! If only we could be as one."

I wish you could see me…

"If you don't hush, I'm going to read to you again. I know how much you hate that."

Don't be afraid…

"Okay. You asked for it. This is called 'The Unexamined Life.' It's something Demery wanted me to try, something I wouldn't do normally. Write from a male perspective. A hard-boiled detective story. My protagonist used to be a cop, but he had a bad experience. I haven't figured out what exactly yet, I don't know if it's crucial to the story. But it was bad, you know. Seriously, life-changing bad. So the guy's quit the force and he's become a beachcomber.

" 'Thirty-eight bucks was a good day for November. A few years back I could have counted on twice that, despite the cold weather, but beachcombing wasn't what it used to be—now all that environmental crap had been mainstreamed, even the dumb-ass crackers who came to Florida to sell Dilaudid and rip off tourists wjp believed in their hearts that it was wrong to litter and tossed their cans and bottles into recycling bins. Fuck a bunch of Greenpeace was my feeling. But thirty-eight bucks was enough to cover my expenses and a couple of drinks, so with dusk coming on, I stowed the metal detector in the van and walked up from the beach to Tuck's Tavern on Main, where I ordered a draft and a shot of well-bourbon.'

" 'It was too early for the evening crowd. The jukebox was quiet; two hookers were playing Ski-Ball in back. The only other customers were an old man wearing an eyeshade and a windbreaker, who seemed to be talking to someone who wasn't there, and sitting directly across from me, this Seminole-looking guy. Big muscular fucker in his thirties, with greasy black hair down to his shoulders and a stolid expression and black markings on his forearms that looked like ants, but I figured must be tattoos. He challenged me to a staring contest, but I ignored him and struck up a conversation with Erroll the bartender. Erroll had flown down to catch the Heat game the night before and was a fountain of insult concerning Shaquille O'Neal's performance. "Typical nigger bullshit" was his capsule review. He then told a racist joke, to which I responded with a polite chuckle. This being America, if you choose not to be friends with racists, you're not going to have a lot of friends, and though Erroll was not exactly a friend, he poured me a lot of free drinks.'

" 'Erroll went back to stocking the well, and I had another look at the guy across from me. His coloration was mostly due, I decided, to the ruddy lighting, and, that in mind, I realized he wasn't a Seminole, but a white guy with a long face and high cheekbones and a deep tan. There was something familiar about him. I didn't put it together right away, but I kept on glancing over at him, and eventually I realized that if you gave him a buzzcut, stripped off thirty-five, forty pounds of muscle, and erased the worry lines creasing his forehead, the frown lines around his mouth, he would greatly resemble my old friend Bobby Bonfleur, who was doing a dime for armed robbery in Raiford. Just the sort of place where a man might acquire muscles, worry lines, and a shitload of tattoos.'

"So what do you think? I'm getting better, huh?"
Silence.
"Yeah, well. I figured that'd be your reaction."

FOURTEEN

Sanie and Jackson haven't had sex for a month, twenty-seven days to be exact, and when he comes to her one rare sunny morning, she's too enervated to deny him. But she's dry as dust down there, dry as the lunar surface, unable to perform this most fundamental of wifely duties, unable to participate in this calendar ritual that, while no longer central to the marriage, nonetheless has occurred once a week for what seems like forever. He's understanding to a fault, solicitous, and pretends it's no big deal. Maybe she's a little under the weather, maybe she should get a check-up. She imagines that when he leaves her to go down to the study, he's bursting to tell her to pick up some lubricant. She's fighting back tears and, after she hears the study door close, she does cry, though God knows it's not about Jackson—he's even less appealing than usual, now that he's letting himself go to seed in his native soil, wearing a scruffy week-old beard, suffering from an outbreak of acne, bathing irregularly, hair curling down onto his unwashed collar. She mops her eyes with a Kleenex, inwardly curses hormones and emotional stress, whatever has called forth this reaction. The thought of Frank Dean crosses her mind, and she cancels it out, *blam!,* she brings down the mental CANCEL stamp right onto that sucker. Even if it weren't simply a sexual attraction, if he was the great love of her life, she doesn't need it, can't use it. She's got a full plate, and he's too much a creature of this place. He's happy in Edenburg and she could never be happy here. But what if he's not happy? Suppose his return was ill-conceived? What then? *Blam!* She puts on jeans and a sweater, forcing her thoughts into a conventional groove. Things to do today. A list. She's a great little listmaker, yes she is. Pick up this, get that fixed, arrange for this, take care of that. By the time she's halfway down the stairs, she's worked herself into a foul mood. She hopes that Allie comes hunting for a spoon today. Allie's avoided her assiduously since their first meeting, but sooner or later she's due for a Sanie-style ass-kicking. So how's it going Anal Intruder-wise? she'll ask. Is that part of Swami Will's tour of the Ass-tral Plane, or does he throw it in extra? And what about that toy action figure? Did he convince you it was an alien probe? She's about to enter the kitchen when the doorbell sounds, a primitive institutional buzzer like those that signal the rolling back of electric gates in a jail. It sounds again, a short burst repeated over and over. Jackson's voice floats out of the study: "Sanie! Will you get that?" Grimly, ready to vent on whoever it turns out to be, she goes to the door and throws it open. "Can I use your phone, ma'am? It's a medical emergency!" A step van is parked in the road, a poster on its side portraying a happy child carrying a glass of water, a sacred glass of water judging by the light radiating from it, and the driver, who's standing on the porch, is short and skinny, his features dominated by a mustache so full, it obscures his upper lip. He wears a pin-striped uniform shirt, the name Sonny embroidered on the pocket. He's agitated, his hands twitching, on the verge of jumping out of his skin. Sanie moves aside, points to the kitchen, and says, "The phone's straight back through that door." It's only after he's rushed past that she realizes he looks familiar, and it's not until she follows him into the kitchen that she recalls where she saw him. The downstairs corridor, the day she did peyote, standing opposite an older man wearing the same kind of shirt, the name Ralph written on his pocket.

"Yeah," he's saying to, she assumes, the 911 operator. "I'll wait just down the road from Snade's. Hurry, okay? No, nobody's with him. My cell phone wouldn't work. I had to drive back and use someone else's." He pauses, then says, "Because, damn it, you ain't never gonna find your way back in there. There's three or four turns you gotta make onto little dirt roads. Now get somebody out here, will ya?" Another pause. "I am calm! I'll wait down the road from Snade's. Please get someone out here!" He bangs down the receiver. "Fucking idiots!" He spots Sanie and says, "I appreciate it," and ducks his eyes, brushing past her on his way to the door. She hurries after him and catches up on the porch. He's lighting a cigarette; his hands tremble.

"Something I can do?" she asks.

"You know where the Turners live? These hippies got this ol' farmhouse way back in the weeds off Payne Road?"

"I'm just visiting. I'm sorry."

"It's okay. I's thinking if you did, you could direct the emergency people where to go, and I could get on back there."

"Sorry. What happened?"

He butts the cigarette on the porch rail, flips the butt into the weeds. "We was making a delivery to the Turners. When they're not home, we're supposed to put the water up in the loft of this rundown old barn they got out back.

So Ralph, that's… he's my friend, he's teaching me the route." His chin quivers and he has to take a moment. "He's going up the ladder balancing these two bottles. Says if I do it a bottle at a time, it'll take all day. Then the ladder give way. He didn't fall far, but I think he's busted up pretty bad. His back's broke, maybe."

"Is there a problem?" Jackson pokes his nose out.

Sanie fills him in and asks if he knows where the Turners live.

"Buncha fucking hippies," Sonny clarifies. "Down there off Payne Road."

Jackson shakes his head. "No. But there's a place… It belonged to a family named Kyle when I was a kid. Will told me a few years ago some college drop-outs had taken it over. If Will were here, he could tell you."

"That might be it," Sonny says. "You take a left onto Payne Road and about mile and half down, you take a right on a trail's hardly more than an old wagon track?"

"Sounds like it could be the Kyle place," says Jackson. "Tell you what, I'll drive down there and if that's it, I may be able to help your friend. I had some medical training in college."

"You wanta take the truck? It gets muddy back in there. I can ride with the ambulance."

"The SUV can handle it." Jackson flicks his eyes toward Sanie and holds out a hand. "Keys?"

Once he's gone, the driver stations himself beside the van, smoking another cigarette, and Sanie closes the door, walks back into the kitchen, where she drops into her customary pose, sitting at the table, her notebook open, looking between the window—a view of the dying cornfield, the woods starting to show drab autumn colors—and the Cumberland Farm Supplies calendar, which she has turned to the September page. Despite the fact that it's thirty years out-of-date, she chooses to pay homage to the passage of time. The picture for September portrays a teenage couple, perhaps a younger, happier version of August's farmer-and-wife (suggesting that time may run backwards in Cumberland Farm Supplies World), strolling hand-in-hand along an oak-shaded country lane, the foliage there in full Super Kodachrome fall regalia. She's confused by Jackson's display of competence, by his willingness to exert himself on a stranger's behalf, though perhaps it's easier for him with a stranger than with someone he knows and purportedly loves. That aside, she marks the fact that the driver, Sonny, was no ghost, and thus it follows that he and his friend Ralph were not ghosts on the day she saw them in the corridor… unless her understanding of ghosts is incomplete, which it well may be. Knowing that the house is haunted has never bothered her, it's never felt threatening. Yet now that something truly strange has happened, something beyond her capacity to name, she feels a cold spot of fear under her collar bone. She opens her notebook, makes a squiggle with the pen, tries to organize her thoughts, intending to write something that will put Sonny and Ralph, Jackson, the world and her place in it into a comprehensible light. A few words that will unsnarl the knot her life has tied in creation. It almost seems possible. After five or ten minutes, she starts the coffee, washes some dishes left in the sink, mindless puttering that serves to chase her uneasiness.

Jackson's back in about an hour. His flip-flops smack the linoleum, striking sharp reverberations from the high yellow ceilings. He tosses the car keys on the counter next to the sink, says, "The guy died," and goes to pour a cup of coffee.

"Was he fiftyish? The man who died?" asks Sanie. "Leathery and tanned? Frizzy hair?"

"His tan had gotten a little chalky by the time I arrived," Jackson says, sitting beside Sanie. "But that basically describes him. Did you know him?"

"I think I saw them in town once. Was he dead when you got there?"

"Yeah." He stirs sugar into his coffee. "You shouldn't let people, strangers, in the house."

Sanie gives him a what-the-fuck look.

"The driver," he says. "You shouldn't have let him inside. He could have been a murderer… or a rapist."

"If he'd been a murderer, not inviting him in wouldn't have stopped him."

"Do you think we should get a chain for the door."

"You want me to pick one up in town?"

She says this sharply, able to restrain her anger, but not to hide it, and, without raising his voice, in a controlled, rational, slightly weary tone, he says, "What would be the point? We're only going to be here another month or so. Don't you think you can be a bit more circumspect? Not invite anyone and everyone in?"

She knows if he had officially suggested that she race into town and buy a chain, he'd be controlled, rational, and slightly weary in support of the idea. His contrariness is designed to make her feel incompetent, though by any practical standard she's infinitely more competent than he. She can do minor repairs on the car, the washing machine; she can deal with the bank, the credit cards, the telephone, all the minor functionaries that plague their lives. He has no need to be competent— he has an entourage of one to handle his affairs. "Anyone and everyone?" she'd like to say. "Have you counted the number of people who've stopped by since we've been here? I have. There've been four. Someone asking for directions, two kids from Furman selling Jesus door-to-door, and Sonny. We're lucky to be alive, we're so besieged by predators."

But she keeps her mouth shut. When it comes right down to it, she does not want to fight, even though she has recognized that she's already in one. She can't abide the idea of a confrontation, and all she wants at the moment is for him to lock himself in his study and leave her alone to collect her thoughts and try to make something of her day. As if he senses this, he says, "Let's drive into town and get breakfast."

"Shouldn't you study?"

"My morning's shot." He stretches luxuriantly. "It'd do me more good to take a few hours off. Re-energize. It'll be nice to spend some time with you for a change."

· · ·

Breakfast is at Nellie's West Side Diner, which seems an incongruous name, because Edenburg isn't big enough to have sides, a knot of streets and houses that a strong thrower could heave a baseball across in three or four tosses. The diner is across from a silo and a freight yard, and is patronized that morning by a couple of short haul truckers, farmers lollygagging over coffee, and, in the booth adjoining Sanie-and-Jackson's, four prosperous-looking old men who speak unintelligibly, talking over one another, like a crowd of extras in a movie who have been instructed to mutter ominously, repeating a phrase like "peas and carrots, peas and carrots..." so as to simulate the rumorous muttering of a mob preparing to break into a jail and hang a rustler. Jackson's in an effusive mood, talking about his high school days, interrupted now and then by their unduly sunny waitress, Marie ("Y'all got everything you need? Well, just holler!"), telling how he won the ninth grade history medal, an event that, in Sanie's estimation, likely solidified his reputation as a geek and caused the rest of his high school career to be miserable, and about his various friends, how they became successful, unlike his various enemies, all of whom remain stuck in Edenburg and environs. Sanie gives stock responses, devotes herself to eating her eggs, knowing if she doesn't, her lack of appetite will inspire a further examination of her health, her behavior. As she's polishing off her orange juice, she notices once again the drastic slide of Jackson's appearance and has a moment of illumination. This trip back to Edenburg, it's Jackson's Rayfield move. He's pulling back from life, giving in to the tension of his elastic band, and he's never going to leave again. Why, she asks herself, hasn't she understood this before? She's been too self-absorbed, she thinks. Too wrapped up in her side of the marital issues to look closely at him. His deteriorating physical appearance is not the only evidence that supports the theory. A regional accent has begun creeping back into his speech, putting cracks into its paved-over neutrality. He's dropping his Gs, using elisions and contractions. His moods are less even. He's acquired disgusting habits like spitting and fondling his balls in public. An easy explanation for all this would be that he's studying for the bar. He's tired, stressed-out, he's let himself go. But that cold spot under Sanie's collarbone has redefined itself, and she knows, she knows!, that Jackson, like Rayfield, is on a slipping-down path from which there will be no turning. The image of Jackson, naked and many-hatted, walking into Snade's, amuses her, but what that signals, distraction and madness (despite Will's testimony, she believes Rayfield was mad), is not amusing in the least, and when Jackson breaks his monologue to have a swallow of coffee, instead of giving the matter due consideration, instead of permitting time and caution to overrule her instincts, she blurts out, "I think we should go back to Chapel Hill."

For once, Jackson is stunned.

"I'll answer the phone," she says. "I'll do everything I can to make sure you're not disturbed."

Poise restored, Jackson takes a bite of egg. "Going home now would be a massive disruption. You'll be back with your friends soon enough."

"It's not about that. It's just I have a feeling…" She falters, wondering how to paint a picture that won't engage his stubbornness any more than is necessary.

"A feeling. I see. A meteor's going to hit the house? This is a Psychic Friends thing, is it? You had a bad dream, like Caesar's wife?"

"Caesar's wife was right," she says. "But no, I didn't have a dream." She takes a breath, hesitates before releasing it. "I've been thinking about leaving you, and I don't know how much of what I feel is due to this place. I want us to go home and take stock."

He stares at her, chewing, and then forks up another bite. He gives a sardonic laugh.

"Saving our marriage is a subject for derision?" Sanie asks.

"No." He draws out the word, as if talking to a child. "I was thinking that you pulling this now is precisely what I needed to help me concentrate."

"The marriage isn't important as the bar—that's what

you're saying?"

"I'm not saying that at all. I'm saying, you want to ruin your life? Go ahead. I'm not going to ruin mine on the slim chance that you're going to do something crazy."

The arrogance of his response, the notion that she'd be ruining her life by leaving him, by abandoning the SUV and the Lexus, the house, all the material perks of the marriage (she knows that's how he views it), and what's more, his arrogance in assuming that she won't leave… It's unbelievable. She's trying to save him from himself, and this is how he reacts? Okay, her first thought is to save herself, but she doesn't want to leave him here to become an unstable old man surrounded by ghosts. At least she's looking out for him. At least that much of her loyalty hasn't been neutralized by years of servitude.

"Are you having an affair?" he asks. "Is that why you want to go home."

Sanie's "no" sounds to her own ears a lot like his. It's how she might deny something when she's lying, and she supposes that she is, in truth, lying—she's been betraying Jackson in her mind for years, and her most recent betrayal has acquired a powerful value.

"This is such a sudden change in attitude," he says. "It's like you've received bad news and need to get back to repair the damage."

"Don't be silly!"

"In light of what happened this morning, I don't think it's silly of me to wonder about another man." He dabs his mouth with a napkin. "I suppose it's not out of the question that you could be trying to end an affair by scurrying back to Chapel Hill."

"Right," she says. "You nailed it. I'm sleeping with our waitress. Cute little, sunny Marie. It's a different thing for me, but so far I'm not hating it."

Apparently hypersensitive to the sound of her name, Marie, who's standing three booths down, starts toward them, snagging the coffee as she comes. Sanie attempts to wave her off, but there's no stopping Marie once her wait-staff reflexes are triggered, and they endure another round of smiles and mug-freshenings.

As he always does, Jackson has turned things around on her, changed the subject and put her on the defensive, and he's preparing to turn it around on her some more, chewing over a new accusation or a follow-up insult, when one of the men from the adjoining booth, a beaming old fart in corduroy trousers and a plaid wool shirt and a gold belt buckle the size of the badge on a county fair ribbon, heaves up beside them and says, "Jackson Bullard? It's not you, is it?"

Jackson allows that it is, in fact, him, and the OF's smile broadens.

"Paulus Haynesworth," he says. "I was a state senator when your daddy was in Colombia. Now I'm not gonna tell you how little you were last time I saw you..." He cocks his head and winks. "But you for sure weren't big enough to be keeping company with a lovely young lady like this." He casts Sanie a fond look, then asks Jackson what he's been up to.

Jackson introduces Sanie, and the two men spend the next minute or ten trading old fartisms, something at which Jackson has become adept, a conversation that ends with Jackson standing and being introduced to the other three OFs, who're settling up with Marie. It becomes a fiesta of back-slapping and haw-hawing. Sanie excuses herself to the ladies room and sits in a stall, wishing she had a cigarette, a joint, something to smooth her out.

She's right about Jackson. He's in trouble and she has to get him back to Chapel Hill. It's not merely loyalty, it's in her self-interest, though it's self-interest in its most responsible form. If she's to make a clean break, she can't have it on her conscience that she left him to go mad. She digs in her purse, recalling the phone number Frank Dean wrote down, and extricates her notebook. The woman who worked for Rayfield. There. Janine Morrison. It's a long shot, but she might provide a piece of information that will help. She digs deeper and strikes gold. At the bottom of the purse, two ten-milligram valium. She usually takes a half, but can't remember how old they are, so she takes both tablets. Swallows it with tap water. Now she's ready to face the drive home.

Jackson, however, doesn't drive straight home. He's over being angry, he's in full-on denial, and he insists upon performing a number of pointless errands in the service of having "fun together." They stop at the drug store, the bakery, the county building, where Jackson visits the records department and has a copy made, and then to the Piggly Wiggly, where he buys her a bouquet, carrying on a cheerful commentary. Sanie doesn't have the energy to play his game. The valium has proven to have lost none of its strength, and when he asks her what's wrong, rather than fabricating a white lie, the manufacture of which has become second nature to her, she's been living a lie so long, all she can think to say is, "I took a valium," and rests her head against the passenger side window, the bedraggled flowers in her lap.

He's silent a few beats, then says, "I thought you were off them."

"I am."

"Yet here you are."

"I found one in my purse and I took it."

"You were looking through your purse, you found a pill, and you said, 'Oh, boy! I'll get wasted.' That's the sort of thing an addict might do."

"Whatever."

"I beg your pardon?"

Sanie closes her eyes on the brick-and-concrete hallucination of downtown Edenburg. "Spin it however you want. Whatever makes you happy."

"I worry about you," he says. "Anti-depressants, valium. You don't ever quit, you just have these intervals between drugs."

Sanie's unresponsive and he goes quiet again. He's so certain nothing's wrong—with him, anyway—and maybe he's right. He's got her half-convinced about half the time that it's all in her head, that if she'll just fix herself, make some adjustment, she will wake to find that everything is hunky-dory and get with the program, support him in his quest to accumulate power, money, and, his latest fixation, a dream house (the last thing she wants is a dream house, a more luxurious prison, a place they'll never have to leave, where they can grow still and old side-by-side, Jackson—in lieu of a pitchfork—holding an immense remote with which he can control everything in their lives, like a hideous yuppie version of *American Gothic*), recognizing that she's part of his accumulation, his little treasure, and accepting this state of affairs. Even now she's tempted toward belief… or not so much belief as surrender. I'll have the lobotomy, Doctor, she'll say, if you promise I won't feel anything afterward. That's the problem with valium. It doesn't make you un-depressed; it only makes you not care that you're depressed.

"I've got one more stop," he says brightly. "After that

we'll get you home."

She nods out for a minute or two, and is roused by Jackson honking the horn. He's parked in front of the collision shop, a cream-colored concrete block building, and Frank Dean is ambling toward them from the service area, wiping his hands on a rag. Sanie has a flutter of panic, wondering what's going on, but it passes. She must look like hell, she thinks. Trashed and clutching these ridiculous flowers. Jackson lowers the window as Frank Dean comes up and Sanie manages a two-fingered wave. After a perfunctory greeting, Jackson asks if they can make an appointment to have the SUV checked out. Change the oil, tune up, and so forth.

"If you want it back same day, better bring it in next week," says Frank Dean. "How about Wednesday morning? Eight, nine o'clock?"

"Wednesday it is." Jackson starts to raise the window, but hesitates and says, "Sanie will probably bring the car in. Could you arrange a ride for her back to the house?"

Frank Dean peers in at Sanie. "Sure. I can run 'er on out."

"Or else…" Jackson looks to her. "You could spend the day in town."

Sanie shrugs. "I'll see how I feel."

"Feeling poorly, are ya?" Frank Dean asks, and Jackson says, "She needs to start taking better care of herself."

"Couple of my workers been out this week," says Frank Dean. "All this rain we been having, I'd be surprised if something wasn't going around."

Ever solicitous, Jackson says to Sanie, "We better get you a flu shot."

Frank Dean peers in at Sanie again, then checks himself and says, "Well, I gotta get on back to work. See ya

Wednesday."

Sanie would like to signal him, to let him know this is being done for his benefit as well as hers, an exercise in control; but she can't think how to do it.

"You bet," Jackson says, affecting a thick accent. "Y'all take care now, y'heah."

FIFTEEN

Judging by her husky voice, Janine Morrison is a woman of some maturity, in her forties at least. She asks how Sanie got her number and when Sanie tells her, she says, "Oh, yeah! I think he mentioned you might call. Isn't he something! I reckon Frank Dean could talk a nun out of being Catholic." She's not adverse to talking about Rayfield, but says her evenings are booked up through next week, and when Sanie suggests lunch, she says, "I work right through my lunch hour so I can get off early." She hems and haws, speaks to someone in her office, and says to Sanie, "Me and some friends are going to the game tonight. You could meet us there?"

"What's the game?"

"It's just high school ball. But Taunton's our main rival, and everybody gets excited when they come to town."

"Will we be able to talk?"

"Not at the game. It's going to be crazy. I was thinking afterward we could stop by Frederick's and talk over a cocktail."

Sanie agrees to this, deciding that she won't try to bargain with Jackson, she'll just get in the car and drive, and deal with him later, because considering all that happened the day before, chances are he'll want to go to the game, if only to make her miserable. She asks how she'll recognize Janine.

"Oh, I'm easy to spot, hon. Look for a big ol' girl with red hair, down front in the Edenburg section. I'll be wearing jeans and a green jersey, and I'll be shaking it all around!"

Sanie lays low for much of the day, avoiding contact, and when contact is impossible to avoid, she avoids meaningful conversation. Jackson essays a probing comment or two over morning coffee, attempting to locate a sensitive spot, but she's shut down emotionally, impervious to his arrows. It's a condition she's sought out with increasing frequency over the years, a kind of flotation device that helps her survive the really bad patches. The marriage has become a eddy that threatens to drag her under, and emotional shutdown allows her to stay afloat temporarily, to bob like a cork and passively resist its pull. She understands that it's a dangerous habit, that she risks it becoming a permanent part of her, and when she's in that mode, she's never at her best, her thoughts churning in sluggish circles. Like today. She knows that Sonny appearing at their door was a sign something is terribly wrong, but as the hours slide past, she loses herself in busy work, sinks deeper into the role of wife, and comes to doubt all of her judgments, no matter how well-founded. They seem flimsy and ridiculous... and then the eddy spins her back around and she bumps into the thought of Sonny and recalls again her reasons for urgency.

After dinner, as soon as she's sure that Jackson is deep in his books, she beelines for the SUV, fires up the engine ,and drives away without a backward glance, fearful that a backward glance might reveal Jackson on the porch and that would be sufficient to stop her. Once she makes the turn at Snade's, however, she's possessed by an extraordinary sense of liberation and, though it's cold for October, she rolls down the window and lets the wind blow out the stale air. It's been a while since she felt this easy in her own skin. Her first glimpse of the field, from a distance, framed by darkness, as if a portal has been punched through into a brighter world where the grass is electric green under banked lights, with tiny figures deployed across a grid of white chalk lines, and the dark benches of the bleachers crowded with the rabid children of Edenburg and Taunton… She pulls the SUV over onto the shoulder and drinks the scene in. Everything appears to be connected by invisible strings, event and reaction coming in an unbroken flow. The players scramble across the field, the crowd roars, a whistle blows, the noise dims, the PA intones. And as this sequence repeats over and over, it begins to seem the expression of a long-buried emotion. No, not an emotion, a way of feeling, of being, that used to be hers before the dirt of the world got shoveled into her eyes, before mold set in and beetles gathered to feed on its decay. Life as a current of hot color and noise in which she could immerse herself anytime she wished.

She arrives at the game early in the second quarter, with Taunton leading 13-7. The Edenburg Pirates, in green unis with white numerals, are playing with energy and skill, but it's only a matter of time, Sanie thinks, before Taunton, dressed in purple jerseys and black pants, wears them down. Their offensive line is enormous, their fullback is bigger than Edenburg's biggest player. Sooner or later, in her estimation, their drive blocking will break the Pirates' will. But in the last seconds prior to halftime, as Taunton's moving downfield toward another score, their quarterback floats a pass, it's a balloon, no zip at all, and number 22, the Pirate safety, leaps in front of the receiver and intercepts, races along the sideline uncontested to the end zone, and Edenburg's up 14-13. The band tootles a discordant version of the fight song; the cheerleaders pogo and hug each other.

During halftime, with the spirit squad doing Rockette kicks on the sideline, Sanie walks past them, scanning the bleachers, the rows of ecstatic Edenburg supporters, and spies a voluptuous redhead in a Pirate jersey. She's been operating under the assumption that "big ol' girl" was South Carolinian for "fat ol' girl," but Janine Morrison, though she's got a few cracks in her veneer, is a good-looking woman with generous features and hair falling to her mid-back, almost six feet tall, sexier and more glamorous (that's the word for her, glamorous, like a movie star from the '40s) than you would think to find grazing in a weedy patch like Edenburg. She welcomes Sanie with a hug, introduces her two female friends, both of whom seem dimmed by her light, less friends than accessories, and says, "We're kicking their ass, huh?"

A one-point lead isn't much of an ass-kicking in Sanie's book, but she keeps her thoughts to herself.

Janine invites Sanie to squeeze on in beside them and then asks, "So you going with Frank Dean now?"

"No!" Sanie's startled by her bluntness. "No, I'm… not. Did he say I was?"

"He didn't have to. Whenever he said your name, he got this sorta gone look." Janine's impression of Frank Dean is gaping and stuporous. "I could see he was smitten with you."

A surge of cheers and band noise attracts Janine's attention—the teams have come back on the field. She picks up a pair of pom-poms, gives them a shake, and begins yelling, "Here we go Pirates! Here we go!" until it builds into a chant.

Edenburg scores quickly after the break and leads 21-13, but thereafter Sanie's analysis proves correct, and Taunton drives for three unanswered touchdowns. The final score, 33-21, does not diminish the crowd's enthusiasm. They cheer loudly until the end and, when a fight breaks out among the players mingling in the middle of the field, they cheer louder yet. Afterward, driving to Frederick's in Sanie's car, Janine tells her this is the closest they have come to beating Taunton in fifteen years.

"Last year the score was forty-four-zip. And a few years back, they put seventy points on our ass," she says. "Hon, you mind if I change into my battle gear?" She yanks the jersey over her head, exposing a pair of large and unsupported breasts. "People round here don't believe much in moral victories." She struggles with the arms. "But this here's one moral victory they'll take." She frees herself from the jersey, stuffs it into her purse, after first removing a skimpy pink top that, to Sanie's eye, won't cover much of Janine's exuberant flesh. But Janine, with much tugging and adjusting, succeeds in making it work, and Sanie has to admit that, though the top is too young for Janine, the result is pretty spectacular.

Frederick's Lounge is upscale for Edenburg, a clean, dimly lit watering hole where black and white families fill the sparkly lime green vinyl booths, eating catfish, pork loin, fried chicken, and hushpuppies. There's a bandstand at the rear, currently unoccupied, and a long bar with poker machines and high-backed stools, about a third of them filled, and a low-key, fairly sedate atmosphere... until Janine bursts through the door, shaking her pom-poms and everything else, shrieking, "Go Pirates!" and then everyone's whooping and waving. Sanie follows in Janine's wake as she stops to hug a half-a-dozen men, feeling like a lady-in-waiting, a little plainer and less vivacious than the queen. They proceed to the rear of the bar, where it's relatively secluded, and, once they've got their drinks (white Russian, Diet Pepsi) and after Janine checks around to ascertain whether or not her entrance created the proper effect, if there is any man left un-hugged, she asks Sanie what she wanted to talk about.

"Rayfield Bullard," says Sanie, surprised that Janine has forgotten, but then she's had so much on her mind: the game, the pink top, men.

"That's right. Good ol' Rayfield! Well, there isn't that much to tell. I worked for him, and he seduced me." She gives Sanie a nudge. "You wouldn't believe the tricks I had to play to get him to make his move. Rayfield may have been a powerbroker in Columbia, but he sure wasn't any kind of a ladies' man. You talk about shy! You'd think the man hadn't never done it before. After the first time, he became more masterful. I must have unlocked his kinky side… and that old devil had some kinks in his tail, let me tell you. But he was so guilty about screwing a woman young enough to be his granddaughter, I had him wrapped around my little finger. He loaned me seed money for my business and cut through the red tape on getting me my realtor's license." Janine flips her hair away from her face and grins at the bartender as he passes. "Being with Rayfield taught me all I needed to know about how to handle men."

Again, Sanie is taken aback by her forthrightness. "Frank Dean told me you had some curious experiences when you were at the house."

"Aside from having sex with Rayfield, you mean?" Janine wrinkles her nose, trying to remember. "You know,

I might have been fibbing. I was hoping to get Frank Dean interested, and I'm liable to say anything when I want something." She says this pridefully, as if it were a virtue.

Disappointed, because the meeting for which she's sacrificed marital peace is proving to be a dud, Sanie falls silent, unable to think what more to ask. A man stops by on his way to the john and hugs Janine, who responds coquettishly, engaging him in a risqué conversation. Once he's gone she turns to Sanie and, as if she's misunderstood Sanie's area of interest, proceeds to lecture her on the psychology of men, a lecture that seems to have been culled from the pages of *Cosmo,* one to which Sanie partially subscribes, yet which seems increasingly general and misguided the more Janine fleshes it out.

"As long as you got the candy, men want it," Janine says. "And that's all a woman needs to know. A girl like you should be out there partying every night and not worrying about what ol' Rayfield was up to."

"I'm married." Sanie flashes her ring.

"You don't have to spell it out in diamonds, Hon," says Janine. "You got a little dark cloud over your head that just screams 'married.' How long's it been? Seven years? Eight?"

Sanie acknowledges that this is in the ball park and is unnerved by the fact that Janine perceives her to be unhappy—Sanie has always thought that she presents an impenetrable smileyface to the world.

Janine goes on, saying, "You know, so many women believe they have issues with men, when all they really have is issues with a *man.* You strip away a man's bullshit, you can have a lot of fun with what's left."

That statement seems to present a contrary to the first

portion of the lecture, and Sanie is about to point this out, when yet another member of Janine's fanclub stops to pay his respects. Hug. Hairflip. This time, the conversation runs long and Sanie fusses with her Diet Pepsi, fiddles with the straw, studies her reflection in the mirror, studies the reflection of the back of the bartender's head. The place is filling with people who were at the game. Somebody feeds the jukebox; an AC/DC tune comes on loud, but is quickly tuned down to a conversation-friendly level. And then (also in reflection) she notices Frank Dean, dressed in jeans and a navy windbreaker, taking a seat next to Janine, who waves good-bye to the other man, hugs Frank Dean, and gives her most dramatic hairflip yet. Sanie refuses to look directly at him. She's almost frozen with anger, guessing that, since Janine and Frank Dean are friends, ex-lovers, or whatever, Janine never had anything of substance to tell her and conspired with him to arrange a "chance" meeting. Staring into the mirror begins to feel stupid and she turns to face them.

"So did Janine help you out?" Frank Dean asks.

"Much to my surprise," says Sanie. "No."

Frank Dean makes a perplexed face and says to Janine, "Didn't you tell her about the horses?"

"Oh my god!" Janine puts a hand to her breast and stares as though horrified at Sanie. "Was that what you meant by 'curious'? That kind of thing?"

Sanie replies that she doesn't yet know to what kind of thing Janine is referring.

"See," says Janine, "that stuff's never seemed extraordinary to me. Ever since I was a little girl, I've had the gift." She bats her eyelashes at Frank Dean. "Not strong, now. Just a touch. But I've always seen things other people couldn't."

"Like ghosts?" Sanie believes that Janine is playing with her, that she knew what Sanie wanted to hear all along and for some reason, probably for the reason in a navy windbreaker sitting next to her, has chosen to make a production out of it.

"If you're asking whether I saw ghosts out at Rayfield's place," says Janine. "Yes, I did. At least I thought that's what they were. But Rayfield told me only some of them were actual ghosts. The manifestations associated with his family. He wasn't even sure about all of them. He used to mark it down whenever he spotted one of his ancestors."

"In a book?" Sanie asks. "I found a composition book with names and dates… "

"You found that old book? Why, that's amazing! I thought all that junk went out the back door when Rayfield died."

"Will saved it." Frank Dean's stare disconcerts Sanie and she has to gather her thoughts. "If Rayfield saw ghosts, he must have had the gift, too?"

"He told me he had a feeling something funny was going on with the house," says Janine. "He didn't see anything, though, until he started taking acid."

Sanie asks, "He didn't use peyote?"

"He experimented with a lot of stuff, 'cause the acid was hard on him physically. I believe he said something about trying peyote, but that was around the time my business took off, and I wasn't really paying attention." Janine pats Frank Dean's hand. "You're being so quiet, Hon!"

Frank Dean shrugs and says something Sanie can't catch. "What about the rest?" she asks just as the jukebox is turned up; the Dixie Chicks' shrill harmonies beat down all other sounds. She has to repeat her question, leaning close to Janine, who's making dance moves on her stool and says, "The rest of what?"

"Say what?"

"The horses! What about the horses?"

"I was out…" The jukebox is turned down again, a happy medium struck, and Janine starts over in a less strident voice. "I was out back, eating lunch at the edge of the woods, and I saw a herd of horses. Thirty or forty of them. They come running through the cornfield straight at me. I swear, I thought they were going to trample me. They were so close I could smell them. I threw myself down in the grass, hoping they'd miss me. And then they were gone. I could still hear their hooves for a while, but they were gone. It happened so fast…" Janine shakes her head as if marveling at her brush with mortality. "Anyway, Rayfield said the horses and a lot of the rest of it, they were related to the vortex. He claimed a vortex was developing around the house."

Sanie says, "A vortex," and Frank Dean says, "A whirlpool?"

"Kinda… but it's energy instead of water." Janine gestures impatiently. "Rayfield said it was getting bigger. I don't know what all it is, really. But I do know it had to be something besides ghosts. Ghosts don't explain some of the things I saw." She catches Frank Dean's hand. "Are you going to dance with me or what?"

"Not right now," he says.

"Well…" Janine slides down off the stool. "*I'm* going to dance."

"What else did you see?" Sanie asks.

"Just more stuff like the horses. I'll fill you in later, Hon." She winks broadly at Sanie. "If you're not occupied, that is."

She dances away along the bar, eyeing the men,

prospecting for a suitable partner, and Frank Dean slides over onto her stool.

"How was the game?" he asks, and Sanie, remembering she's angry, says, "Great."

She stares at a poker machine mounted on the bar, fishes out her coin purse, slots in a quarter, and grimly punches up a hand. Not even a pair. She draws four cards and loses.

"So how you been?" asks Frank Dean.

Sanie pops another quarter into the machine. "Fine." She wins two free plays.

"Why're you mad at me?"

"I don't like being set up." She punches up another losing hand.

"What're you talking about?"

"I'm talking about I arrange a meeting with Janine…" She draws a straight, stands pat. "And you just happen to turn up." The machine beats her with a full house.

"I've been worried about you."

"You don't know me. How can you worry about me?"

She cuts her eyes toward him so as to see what damage she's inflicted. His face tightens, but remains impassive. She feeds the machine again. Four hearts and a spade. She makes her flush and wins five free plays.

"The other day, when you came by the shop," he says, "you were in rocky shape. I know you're not happy. I can…"

"You sensed my unhappiness, did you? And you thought, what that girl needs is a shot of Frank Dean? A little push-push where it'll do the most good? Does that about sum it up?"

Bonnie Tyler is having a Total Eclipse of the Heart and, ordinarily, Sanie would swing around and scornfully observe the white folks trying to dance to the slow section, bending and swaying like time-lapse photography of plants dying; but she, too, is having an eclipse, albeit one unaccompanied by soaring strings and a boys choir: the sun of sexual attraction obscured behind the moon of her anger at the World of Men.

"Can't we talk about this calmly?" asks Frank Dean.

Sanie laughs, and the laugh feels as if it's going to keep unfurling, like one of those endless scarves favored by clowns and magicians. She bites it off and says, "Why's it the only time men resort to reason is when they're being rejected? Women are much more realistic. They go straight to crazy." She spins around, her knees bumping his. "There is no 'this' to talk about. Hell, we don't even have a 'that.'"

He looks at her steadily, gravely, as if framing a weighty response, and says, "We did so have a 'that.'"

She can't help herself, she laughs, and puts a fist to her forehead and closes her eyes. "God! Yes, we had a 'that.' I admit it."

"I'm not looking to get over on you," he says. "All I want…"

Janine comes huffing up and sags against him, again urging him to dance, and he says, "In a minute. We're still talking."

She defines the verb "flounce" as she goes petulantly off, and Frank Dean says, "If you need a place to stay, I want you to call my sister. She's got a huge house and nobody else lives there. Alice Settlemyre. She's in the book."

"What are you talking about? I don't need a place to stay."

"You might. Marriages can get ugly. People try and hurt each other however they can."

"Jackson wouldn't hurt me."

"I got a feeling he hurts you plenty. Maybe you've hurt him, too. I don't know. But nobody deserves some of the shit can rain down in a marriage. Especially the physical shit."

Sanie half-swings back to the poker machine. Does everyone see what she cannot? They certainly seem able to see what she believed was hidden behind a cheerful facade.

"He wouldn't hit me," she says. "I'm certain of that."

"Maybe you haven't given him a reason to hit you. That could change."

"No. It's not in him. And even if he were like that, I'm tougher than him. Smarter, too."

"I bet you're more trusting than him. That might cancel out those other qualities." Frank Dean lays a hand on her shoulder. "Alice Settlemyre. I'm just saying… Okay? If you need it."

"Were you married?"

He grimaces. "Yeah. It was bad."

"Did you… hurt your wife?"

"I hurt her. Yeah. Not physically, though. That was all on her." He pulls down the neck of his T-shirt, exposing a puckered round scar below his collarbone.

"She shot you?"

"Twice. Got me in the hip as I was falling. Then the gun jammed."

"Was she…" Sanie falters, unsure what question would be safe to ask.

"Crystal meth," says Frank Dean. "She was crazy as a shithouse rat. She claims I drove her to using. I suppose she's right… at least part."

Having made this confession, he seems less imposing, a

working man worn down by his day.

"I'm sorry," she says. "Is that why you left LA?"

"I blamed LA. That was a mistake. It wasn't LA. It was this special poison we brewed for each other. We would have done it anywhere."

"So now you wish you were back in LA?"

"There was a time I did, but now… I'm okay with it. Only thing LA had going was I could make more money there. Sometimes that seems important, but… you know. My head's better off here." He exhales forcefully and stretches his back. "I should get on home before Janine comes back at me. I don't have the energy to deal with her tonight."

"She's a trip, all right," Sanie says.

"She's a good woman. Little man-crazy's all."

He drops a dollar on the bar, pockets the rest of his change, and Sanie reaches out to restrain him, not wanting to be left alone, not yet inclined to return home, having a flashback to how she felt that rainy day in the coffee shop. And then she notices Jackson. He's standing on the dance floor, right at the edge, about ten feet away, impeding the moves of a middle-aged couple doing their best to rock out to Springsteen. Will's at his shoulder, playing Hyde to his Jekyll—that's how Sanie sees them, as halves of the same person, the Bullard male. For an instant she wants there to be trouble. A seam of viciousness is exposed, and she wants Frank Dean, who's become aware of Jackson, to wipe the floor with him; but as Jackson steps toward them, she says, "Go, go!" and pushes Frank Dean away.

Frank Dean says, "You be all right?" and she says, "Yes, just go!" He hesitates, and she shoves him harder. "Please go!"

Jackson says something as Frank Dean brushes past him

and, when Frank Dean fails to react, Jackson throws a punch at his back that glances off the shoulder. Frank Dean stops, his face cinched with anger, but his eyes contact Sanie's and he starts to walk away. Jackson wraps his arms around him from behind, trying to wrestle him down, and, as the Boss launches into the chorus of "Glory Days," as the dancers mass together and give the combatants room, displaying the same fixity and exultation with which many of them watched the game, Frank Dean breaks free and nails Jackson with two body punches that double him over, grabs him by the hair, lifts his head, and cracks him in the face with such force that Sanie hears the blow land. Jackson sags, but Frank Dean hauls him upright and cracks him again. Jackson slides to the floor and rolls onto his back. The violence… It's so mechanical, such an efficient destruction, it doesn't seem representative of the passions involved. Frank Dean stares at Sanie for a long moment, his expression revealing regret, bitterness, anger, hopelessness, and then he bulls through the crowd toward the door.

The crowd's no longer interested in Jackson, who comes to his hands and knees, hanging his head; their attention is all on Sanie, waiting for her to show her colors, to assist Jackson or run after Frank. She's not sure what she's going to do, but she comes to her feet and, through force of habit if nothing else, kneels by her husband. Blood drips from his face onto the floor. Numbly, she puts a hand on his back, asks if he's okay. Will tugs at Jackson's arm, and the bartender is there, too, helping him stand. Together, they walk Jackson toward the door, but after a few steps he shakes them off and goes on his own, with Sanie following. The chorus of "Glory Days" begins its fade, and she can hear people murmuring, some doubtless asking what happened and others, eager to spread the story, saying how it was all on account of that Sanie girl, the one who used to stroll around town wearing next to nothing, that Frank Dean spilled the blood of Rayfield Bullard's prodigal son.

. . .

Though his left eye is swelling shut and his nose won't quit bleeding, Jackson insists on driving the SUV back to the house. Sanie straps in tight beside him, worrying that he's concussed and will have an accident. She tries to talk him into going to the emergency room of Edenburg's tiny clinic, but he refuses to respond; in fact, he refuses to speak at all for the first minutes of the ride. The black miles roll by, their headlights rearranging the emptiness. Finally he says, "I'm not going to ask if you're sleeping with him. I know you are."

Sanie presses her cheek to the cold window and says, "I'm not sleeping with anybody."

"Nobody you're married to," he says. "That much is certain."

Guilt nuzzles at her, but she's too spent to indulge the feeling, and she's not interested in continuing the argument.

"I understand I haven't always given you the attention you deserve," he says. "And perhaps I deserve this. But your choice of men really disturbs me. First there was that little art fag back in Chapel Hill, and…"

"Art fag? What are you talking about?"

"Howard. Howard the art fag."

"He's my friend! He helps me with my writing."

"I'm sure he does. I'm sure he tells you what a sensitive creature you are. I've read his emails. They're infantile foreplay."

He swerves to avoid roadkill on the shoulder, a large bloody shape of indeterminate nature. A werewolf, Sanie thinks. Or a minotaur. Fabulous creatures are springing out from the South Carolina darkness, coming down to drink and die on the banks of the new River Lethe, State Road 226.

"That one email about his influences." Jackson continues. "That was my favorite. 'Baudelaire spoke to my soul, and I believe he would speak to yours as well, Sanie.' And there was one… I think it went like this." He adopts a high-pitched adenoidal voice. " 'The dark slants of the Bard's humor conjure magic from the most banal circumstance.' I bet that one got you juicy."

Sanie's guilt evaporates. "So what you're telling me, if I was fucking a better class of guy, you wouldn't object? I'll start bringing them home for your approval."

"Do you think that would work? I don't know. You seem drawn to certain types. If you were a car, you'd have a bumper sticker on your front that read, 'I brake for art fags.' And on the rear, 'I heart Neanderthals.'"

"So which category do you fall into?"

"Husband," he says. "I'm the one who earns your… your *favors*. But I don't receive them except as grudging installments. Always late, always a few dollars short."

She has the urge to offer mock applause and, affecting a cultured British accent, say, "Wonderful metaphor! Well turned! And spontaneous, too! Born of the moment. Not at all practiced-feeling." Yet she's shocked by his comment—it's the closest he's come to admitting that something is wrong, and she wonders if now might be the time to get their problems out in the open. But the opportunity is lost. He's on a roll, he starts taking her apart, telling her verities about herself that she's unable to deny, spinning them to make her seem calculating, treacherous, not maltreated, and making himself out to be long-suffering, patient, a reasonable man—flawed, to be sure—tied to an unreasonable woman who doesn't respect him, who's ungrateful for the cushy life he's provided. His words hold enough truth to confound her, to cause her to doubt once again her view of the marriage. Something, she thinks, must have happened early in life to bind them to this fate. Were their feet tied together with black string when they were babies and a cabalistic spell muttered? Were leaf-painted Druid mirrors holding their infant reflections shattered at the same instant, while they drooled happily in cribs miles apart? It can't be simply a matter of human weakness. Some woeful magic must be involved, the union is that durable, its tensile strength enormous, like the stuff of an otherworldly element, one kept secret from the world in the Vatican vaults or buried in Henry Ford's grave.

He starts in on her father, not saying anything outright, but suggesting a link, questioning whether he might have provided the template for Sanie's erratic character, listing his faults, his alcoholism, gambling, liberal causes, his trivial mind, his casual attitude toward his various responsibilities, going on and on until Sanie wishes for the accident she originally feared, Jackson passing out, the SUV arrowing toward the gas pumps at Snade's Corners, the luscious finality of the impact, the gasoline erupting into a ball of flame bigger than the store it's consuming.

"Stop it," she says. "Just stop it."

He glances over, a look of surprise on his battered face, illuminated briefly by the lights of a passing pick-up, and she sees what a job Frank Dean did on him: the left side of his forehead and cheek swollen along with the eye; a cut around the eyebrow, blood still trickling. She imagines his surprise is due to the deadness in her voice, which has surprised her as well, and she notes that he hasn't mentioned Frank Dean other than obliquely in all this long rant.

"We're going to talk about this later," he says. "And you're going to listen."

SIXTEEN

Midafternoon, the day after the bar fight, Jackson's sequestered in the study, the promised talk has not materialized, and Sanie's drinking vodka straight from a plastic jug she bought at Snade's. Not drunk, but getting there. She's standing naked in front of the full-length mirror in the bedroom, an oval mirror set in an antique frame of cherrywood gone dark with age. She turns in profile, examining the jut of her breasts, thinking that they're still firm and high enough to pass the pencil test—she looks around for a pencil to place under a breast and see if it falls. Finding none, she has another drink and examines her rear end. Cellulite-free. On the whole, a top-notch butt. Cute, yet sufficiently full and womanly.

Facing front, she's more critical. She's let her pubic hair grow into an unruly patch because it grosses Jackson out, but that's easily fixable. What bothers her is the lack of symmetry. She recognizes that the human body is slightly asymmetrical. One breast a little larger, one foot, one hip, one everything. Yet her asymmetry is such, she resembles a Cubist woman. She can't isolate the cause, can't determine which of her features is throwing her so ridiculously out of balance. She pictures herself with a single enormous eye and a thigh the approximate mass of a cow's. It's almost that bad. She places the vodka bottle on the floor and straightens up. That's better. She adopts a Bangles-style Egyptian pose. Hieroglyph woman. That's better yet. She slides her right hand down over the swell of her abdomen, dips a finger into the dark tangle and finds her clit. Her eyelids flutter, half-shutting, and that perfects her. She's desirable in sum once again. She should have known—it's a lack of perception that orders the world. She twitches her finger away from the sensitive area, dismissive of pleasure. She doesn't want to feel anything today. She stoops to pick up the bottle, but leaves it there and sits at the foot of the bed. If she senses herself growing asymmetrical again, she can lean to the right and check her reflection in the mirror. She lies back, fumbles for her purse beside the bed, and grabs her cell phone. Brittany. She'll call Brittany. She gets voicemail and switches the phone off, realizing that Britt must be ducking her calls. She tries to think of someone else, but her options are limited. Howard… but he can't talk at work. A couple of women and a man with whom she has coffee regularly, members of her writing group. But they're not intimates and she can't predict how they would react if she were to confide in them. Roll their eyes and get off the phone as quickly as they could, no doubt, so they could call their real friends and gossip. In their eyes, she knows—she supposes, anyway—she's a talentless dilettante for whom writing is a hobby, and they think if they're nice to her, they may be able to con her into funding one of their projects with Jackson's money. Rock bottom, there's Mom, but she prefers not to hear a lecture. The friends list on her blog is extensive, but they're not friends, they're co-conspirators in bloggery, a form of sham acquaintance. Friends Lite. She recalls a meme she suggested on the blog: Suggest Three Things You Can Imagine Us Doing Together (G-Rated Only!).

The responses were boring. Watch a football game. Have coffee in New York. No one suggested anything daring, anything that would require imagination or commitment. Which suggests that she has become boring, that no one perceives her to be a committed, imaginative person. This despite the fact that, while a teenager, she spent two summers in Africa working with children on a church project. That alone should make her not-boring, in addition to committed, because Africa was far from boring and required a significant commitment. It's the main reason she originally wanted to write, to talk about her time there… Anyway, now that Brittany has virtually abandoned her, there's only Howard, and though he would commiserate, she doubts he'd be able to offer advice on a crisis. If it is a crisis. If it isn't all in her head, as was the case with her asymmetry. She shifts to the right, squares up in front of the mirror. Breasts of more-or-less equal size and perkiness. Cunt tucked primly away between proportionate thighs. She tips her head to the side, smiles. The Mary doll. Just hook on a paper dress and blouse. Or not. A great gift for the guy in your life. She cooks, she cleans, she crawls on her belly like a reptile… She heaves up from the bed, changing into a tipsy, unsmiling woman, crosses to the bureau, takes a pair of panties from the top drawer and slips them on. A shirt from the bottom drawer. She no longer wants to risk nudity. Jackson may catch her unawares and think it an invitation. She scoots into her jeans and red Skechers and goes downstairs, half-falling into the door at the bottom. She opens it and feels like she has descended into the tropics. She inspects the thermostat in the hall.

"Did you mean to set the heat this high?" she calls out to Jackson, who's shut away in his study. "It's eightysomething."

"Leave it alone!" he shouts.

"Why's it so high?"

"It makes my face feel better! All right?"

What a crock! She snatches a jacket from the hall closet and goes out, slamming the door behind her.

She strides briskly down the muddy road to Snade's, burning off her buzz. Drizzly skies and desolate fields. A crow flaps down to perch on a broken fence, pecking at its ragged feathers. Along the roadside, she can make out every flattened can, faded label, bit of broken glass, every condom, used tissue, diaper, newspaper, and drinking straw. All come out to show themselves from under summer's green, ringing in the season of spoilage, replacing the weeds and flowers. It's almost festive. She paints a picture of imps with zircon-colored wings, armored toadlike creatures belching methane, lovers dawdling in candy-wrapper hammocks, shrunken gray warriors with spears fashioned from those plastic Burger King thingys that pin pickles to Whoppers, a world of faerie appropriate to the day, secreted under mushrooms and within beer-can keeps, preparing to celebrate the Mid-Autumnal Eve… She puts the brakes on this train of thought. Naturalism, she reminds herself. "Observe the world," Professor Demery has cautioned her. "Don't riff on it." He doesn't care for the fantastic. But then she tells herself, Fuck Demery. Fuck naturalism. If she's ever going to be more than a workshop junkie, it's time she followed her own instincts. And if that leads her into the forbidden area of pollution festivals and candy-wrapper love hammocks, so be it. It's possible that in "disciplining her gift," as Demery puts it, she's been restricting her imagination as rigorously as Jackson restricts her movements, letting her out only in channels he deems proper. For all intents and purposes, her writing teacher has served as Jackson's assistant, helping fit a governor to her brain.

She stomps up the stairs to Snade's porch, scrapes her muddy shoes, bangs through the screen door. Usually on Saturday afternoons, Gar's buddies, Sammy and Carl Jr., join him to watch football on the portable TV he keeps behind the counter, but today he's by himself, gloomy as the October weather, poor ol' balding plug of a country boy, hands folded on his dumpling belly, sitting in a lawn chair behind the counter, alone with his canned peas and frozen dinners and coolers full of Bud Light and Heine, beer froth clinging to his Fu Manchu. She asks where Sammy and Carl Jr. are, and he says, "Beats me." He starts to say more, pulls it back, and then says, "Truth be told, we had a falling-out."

"That's too bad." She points at the TV. "Who's playing? Bama?"

"Georgia-Bama. Bama's up by three." He brightens. "Gamecocks whupped Tennessee again."

"Fucking Spurrier," says Sanie.

Gar looks as if he's impressed by her use of profanity. "Man can coach, sure enough."

"And Fullmer can't game-coach a lick." Sanie takes a Diet Pepsi from the cooler. "Mind if I watch a while."

"Pull up a stool."

They watch the end of the second quarter, separated by the counter, making football noises: "Did you see that!" and "That boy like to tore him in half!" and such. A camaraderie having been established, Sanie inquires as to the nature of Gar's falling-out with Sammy and Carl Jr.

"It was my fault, I reckon," Gar says. "We got real drunk watching the Gamecocks and Vandy last week. Game wasn't for shit and we went through about three twelve-packs. I got to thinking, I ain't nothing but free beer to those two. They been coming in for years, and not just on Saturdays. There's NFL and weekday games. Hell, bowl season, they're in almost every day. I started toting it up, and I figured they must have drunk thousands of dollars worth. It's been four or five years since either one of 'em paid for anything. Chips, Slim Jims, and what-all. I made mention of the fact. I know them boys haven't got a pot to piss in, but 'least they could do is bring me by some of that shine they cook up." Gar pauses for a breath. "Anyhow, they didn't take it too well."

"They'll be back," says Sanie.

"I don't know if I want 'em back, that's the way they're going to be." Gar heads for the cooler and grabs a Bud Light. "It's a matter of principle. A relationship ought not to be all one-sided."

Sanie thinks she should advise Gar that it wasn't one-sided, that he derived from it the benefit of Sammy-and-Carl Jr.'s company; but she wonders if she's qualified to offer advice, if she has not been playing Sammy-and-Carl Jr. to Jackson's Gar. Or perhaps vice-versa. It's a stretch, yet there are correspondences.

"You guys'll work it out," she says.

"It's up to them," he says, sitting back down. "I ain't lifting a finger. As it stands, things are going to go a lot better with my wife when I don't come home stinking drunk."

"Maybe you should think about what you were getting out of the relationship and set a value on it. That might help you make a decision."

Gar's brow furrows. "Yeah, maybe." He unscrews the cap of his fresh beer. "You know, I don't want you to take this wrong, because I like having company for a game, but you don't never stay this long. Is something wrong at home? I heard about the mix-up at Frederick's."

"No," she says in reflex; then, because she senses a sliver of genuine concern beneath his raw curiosity, she adds, "I guess you could say Jackson and I had a falling out, too. It's no big deal."

Gar eyes her briefly, sucks on a tooth. "Well, if you need anything, you give a shout, y'hear."

She knows he means that if there's any trouble at the crazy Bullard house, give a shout, and thinks that she should be insulted; but his concern, shallow as likely it is, warms her.

The game turns into a punting contest in the second half, and Sanie has difficulty paying attention to it, weighty problems crowding out her dull enjoyment. This time, she swears, she won't let things continue. That's what Jackson wants, to continue, to pretend Frederick's was a speed bump, to continue to pretend, to pretend to continue. This time, she intends to bring things to a head. She won't allow herself to lapse, to slide back into routine. She's going to find out if there's any truth to this crap about a vortex; she's going to pry Jackson out of here and get him back to Chapel Hill before he turns into Rayfield. And then she's going to leave him. Once he passes the bar, she'll unhook her paper dress, her doll clothes, and slip away. Gar says something that doesn't penetrate her fog and she asks him to repeat it as he heads for the cooler.

"I think what you said might be right," he says. "About friends not being what they used to be."

Bewildered, she doesn't recall saying anything of the sort.

"About them not being worth what they once was," he says.

He appears to have taken her advice in a peculiar

direction, or maybe he's a savant, a genius bumpkin, and has made a leap into the core of her advice and mined a fresh truth. In the devalued culture, a devalued truth about a devalued people, yet no less true.

"Right," she says.

Gar opens the cooler and tosses her a Diet Pepsi. "I appreciate it."

SEVENTEEN

She dreams she's in a firefight, but not with Jackson, not unless it's a metaphorical firefight, and, on waking, she doesn't believe that it was. A metaphorical dream would have lasted longer, had a coherent structure, been heavy on identifiable symbols. This was short, chaotic, and nasty, without apparent structure or symbol—a skirmish at dusk in an open-air building with countless stalls, gutters in the concrete floor, like a city market in Africa. She was firing on the run at blue-white muzzle flashes, and people were dying around her. The enemy's fire made a different sound from hers. *Phut phut phut.* Like mortar rounds, but softer. When the rounds struck, they ripped off arms and legs, excavated chests and bellies. She crouched behind a bin—a spill of water on the floor reeked of fish—and peered out into the aisle. Half-obscured by the bin across from her lay a body. She couldn't make out whether it was a man or woman, friend or enemy. It was too dark. She could barely see the shape of the body rising like a rumpled island from the blood pooled around it.

That was all of the dream, all she can remember, anyway. It didn't have the feel of an anxiety dream. Though her situation was desperate, though she felt some anxiety, she wasn't agitated; she was searching for avenues of escape, analyzing the situation as might an experienced soldier, and she thinks now that a dream like this might be a slice of another life, one lived in another part of the plenum, come to her in a time of need, urging her to analyze and to act.

So perhaps it was a metaphor.

She lies in bed until nine, showers and dresses, then goes to Will's door and listens. A man's voice, a feminine giggle. Sanie knocks. The voices fall silent. She knocks a second time, louder. "Will," she calls. "I have to talk to you."

"I'll be down in a while!"

"Now! I want to talk now."

She doesn't think he's going to respond, but then she hears him, rummaging, shuffling toward the door. He opens it a crack, posing an unappetizing picture with his mussed hair, pasty complexion, and brown silk robe, gazing sullenly at her. The smell of sex accents the customary odor of mildew and filth that issues from within.

"Why didn't you tell me about the vortex?" she asks.

His sullenness departs, confusion fades into view. "I... uh... It wasn't important, didn't seem."

"Not important? It's the reason why the house is so weird. At least, according to your daddy."

"I guess..." He glances over his shoulder. "I'm sorry. I should have said something."

"What exactly is a vortex?"

"Will?" Allie's sugary voice wafts through the crack. "You two're going to talk, let her come on in."

"What about... I mean, you want to..."

"It's all right. I don't mind, if she doesn't."

Will stares foolishly at Sanie, what seems a mixture of pride and embarrassment in his face, and steps back to admit her. At the heart of Will's ratty nest, its milky treasure, Allie lies on the bed, naked and spread-eagled on her belly, breasts squashed beneath her, a pillow placed under her hips to elevate her fleshy buttocks, hands and feet tied to the bedposts with ropes of black velvet.

"Hello!" Allie half-sings the word.

Sanie is certain that her reactions are in plain view, that a measure of consternation has surfaced in her face and body language; she tries to cover it and says, "Allie." Affecting nonchalance, she sits in one of the mauve armchairs.

"Francine," says Allie. "Call me Francine."

"Fine," says Sanie. "Francine."

"We're play-acting," Allie explains. "And I wish to remain in character. I'm Francine, a Belgian submissive of the eighteenth century, and Will's the…"

"I can imagine," Sanie says.

Allie makes a disapproving moue, but holds her tongue. Will sits in the other armchair, carefully tucking in his robe so as to cover his privates. His eyes flick back and forth between the two women, and Sanie thinks he must be picturing a threesome.

"So," she says. "The vortex."

Will scratches the back of his neck, doubtless infested with eighteenth-century cooties. "There's a bunch of theories, but they're bullshit mostly, I figure. A weak point in the fabric of time and space, where energy flows between the dimensions… or universes. Between here and the hereafter. All I know is there's an energy here you can't find nowhere else." He kicks at one of the magazines on the floor. "I got some articles somewhere about vortexes, but they won't tell you more than what I just did."

Allie corrects him. "Vortices, not vortexes."

"People say all kinds of shit," Will says, ignoring her. "They put you in touch with elves and fairies, Indian spirits. But they just saying that to make a buck."

"The vortices in Sedona," Allie says. "Y'know, in Arizona?"

"Rayfield said the vortex was developing," Sanie says.

"They're supposed to be quite salubrious," says Allie primly. "I'd like to…"

"If you're going to play a submissive, Francine," says Sanie, "act submissive."

A frown mars Allie's brow, but only for a second or two. She makes a faint "ooh" noise and wriggles contentedly in her bonds.

"Rayfield seems to be suggesting that this vortex is growing, getting stronger," Sanie goes on. "Doesn't that worry you?"

"Why would it? This is our home," Will says. "Our place. Nothing here's going to do us any harm."

"It may already have harmed you."

Will blinks. "I don't… What you mean?"

"Pardon me for saying so, but your family has certain peculiarities." Sanie holds up a hand to forestall Will's attempt to interrupt her. "However you spin it, you can't deny you and Louise are a little off-center. And Rayfield… I don't care what anybody says, he was a nut. Look at Jackson. He's tried to be normal for so long, he's all knotted up inside. And now he's pulling a Rayfield. He's settling in. It won't be long before he starts flapping a bedsheet at lights in the sky, trying to contact the mother ship. Don't you think the vortex might have something to do with that?"

"May I speak?" Allie asks.

Will beats Sanie to it and says, "No!" He scratches his neck again, runs a hand through his hair, begins to speak, stops. Finally he says, "My granddaddy was an orderly soul his whole life. Married to the same woman forty years.

Went to church every Sunday. There wasn't a single thing he ever did people'd call weird."

"Well, that supports what Rayfield said," Sanie says. "Maybe the vortex wasn't strong enough to affect your grandfather, but by when Rayfield was born, maybe it had gotten strong enough to affect a baby."

Will mulls this over. "You think Jackson's doing what my daddy did?"

"Yeah, I do. I can't be a hundred percent sure, but that's what I think."

"I expect…" Will does some more blinking and scratching. "I expect we ought to help him, then."

"That's what I'm trying to do. But I need *your* help."

"Sir William!" Allie half-sings her dialogue again, sounding like a senile old lady calling to her cat.

Will waves her to silence. "In a minute." He scuffs the floor with his foot, inadvertently opening a magazine with a flying saucer on the cover. "What you want I should do?"

"Give me some of your peyote," Sanie says. "I need to see the vortex."

"Why?"

"When I talk to Jackson, I have to be convincing. I have to know what I'm saying is true. It'll take a hard sell to persuade him."

Will struggles with the idea. "Peyote's not for everybody."

"I've done acid," Sanie says, not wanting to admit she's stolen from him. "The last time was years ago, but I didn't have a problem."

"I don't know."

"Please! I've got to do this."

"You can't always see it," Will says. "Not unless it's in

a strong cycle. It don't always run strong."

"Come on, Will. I don't know if I believe in this thing. I'm sorry, but I can't trust what you're telling me… and the person who told me about it originally, I can't trust her, either. I want to see for myself."

"All right." He gives a complaining noise as he stands. "You're lucky today's overcast. The clouds make it easier to see. Best place to see it's from the edge of the woods. You know where the woods fall away about fifty feet behind the house? It's like a notch? Get back in the notch."

He doles out seven gray-green buttons from his box— they look deadlier than before, like little armor-plated bulbs from the Cretaceous—and, when she asks if she needs to take them all, he says, "You said you wanted to see it, right?"

Feeling imperiled now that she has gotten what she asked for, she's suddenly frightened of the drug, of what she'll have to endure, the foul taste, the poisons. Doubts crowd in, but she refuses to let them possess her. Whether she's crazy or the Bullards are crazy, this is the only way she can think to get a line on the vortex. Still, she tries to delay the experience, asking Will if he and Louise can do anything by way of influencing Jackson. He assures her that they will do their very best. Lingering by the door, she says, "Y'all have fun, now." And then, addressing herself to Will, making a pale joke, adds, "If you untied her, you might have more fun."

Will appears to be giving the idea a turn, but the submissive, slightly miffed, is adamant in her rejection. "Personally," she says, "I prefer a strong hand."

EIGHTEEN

Out in the November chill, Sanie's mind goes tumbling and she isn't sure she'll be able to focus on anything. Seven buttons turns out to be a potent dose, and why not? It's almost half-again what she took the last time. And these are special buttons, hand-selected by Sir William, the Master of Boom-Boom. She breaks a rank sweat and sheds the winter coat she's bundled up in, not because it's too warm, but because its thickness, its weight, is controlling her. She can't get comfortable for more than seconds at a time, whether sitting or standing. She walks around for a while, but that makes her dizzy and upsets her stomach, which is bloated and hard as a cantaloupe. Even after she pukes violently over some twigs of which someone—Will, most likely—has constructed a tiny fort at the foot of an oak tree, she wants to puke more, and she doesn't start to feel better until she moves farther into the woods, away from the house.

The woods are actually no more than a stand of locust and hickory and ironwood, some blackjack oaks on the fringe, and one lone willow, that separates the Bullard property from a working dairy farm. It only covers a handful of acres, but despite this, despite the barren trees, a few red and brown leaves left clinging, at its center it seems mysterious and deep, with the heavy scents of damp, rotting vegetation, the dripping quiet nicked by her twig-snapping footsteps, the thick mulch of dead leaves, the slow push of gray-dark clouds across the lower sky. She marvels at their complexity, how their edges breed tendrils, wisps that evolve and coalesce with such particularity, she can detect the particles of dust and moisture that comprise each delicate shift. Pattern is everywhere, of course. The world is an infinite mosaic overlay—look closely, peer down through the patterns of leaf, bark, mold, and dirt, and you might eventually arrive at a comprehension of the Grand Design; but she's not into patterns, she's impatient to explore the woods and she wanders among the trees, between the gates of their rain-slickered trunks. There are gates everywhere, too—one tree forming a gateway with the next, and so forth, and, as she passes through each, she senses that she is changing, that her edges are dissolving and coalescing into new forms. Her toes turn up beetles and bait worms, a shard of red plastic, a rusted key to no door, a headless action figure, toadstools with empurpled tumescent caps that crumble when they're nudged, revealing a chambered flesh, the penis everywhere, she'll write a poem someday... but she doesn't stop to look at them, she pushes on across the lower sky, breeding a new Sanie from the cloud-smoke of the old.

She begins to notice crows high in the branches. They creep her, there are so many. She counts to fifty-eight and gives up, because they're vibrating too rapidly to look at—when she stops the count, she finds they no longer unnerve her and tells herself there's a larger lesson in that, but it's one she knows intuitively, and thus she doesn't pursue it. At the foot of an ironwood tree, one in whose smooth, muscular bark and twisted limbs she perceives a female torso with arms upflung, imprisoned or incapable of movement, awaiting the formation of legs to split from the fathering trunk… Two crows are perched close together in that tree, sharing a branch, and the eyes of the bigger crow appear made of dull silver. She imagines if she were to give a sign, perform an obeisance, it would counsel her or drop some divine token that, in itself, would be a counsel. Yet though she's tempted to believe the crow is a spirit, it's not the sort of totem she can accept; she has too cynical a cast of mind to credit nature with the capacity to manifest such a creature.

She assumes she's lost, but she emerges from the trees very near where she entered them and shortly after her encounter with the silver-eyed crow, as if by her rejection of it, her right to be in the woods has been revoked, her adventure terminated. She finds her coat, bundles up again—she's cold and welcomes its constricting weight. She gulps down water from a bottle tucked in a side vent, sits and inspects the packet of bread and cheese she's brought, but decides she's not ready to eat. She glances at the house. No vortex. Just the wind currents, visible as translucent swirls against the churning, mud-ugly sky. She pinches the collar tightly about her throat and shivers. The shiver seems to run out of her into the earth, where it joins a profound trembling, a vibration that never ceases, and she's purged again, this time of cold. Calmness fills her, like she's a jug held under the surface of a stream. Rather than seeking out experience, she allows it to come to her. The remnants of the cornfield file away to her horizon, strands of cornsilk showing as silver-gray braid against the sere, darkened husks, the stalks all broken and bent akimbo—she imagines if she could see the entire field from above, it would present a pictographic record of the place. Gray shadow cats with gleaming green eyes slalom around the stalks, moving along the separate rows, weaving in and out, disappearing when they draw near, then reappearing at the far ends of the rows and beginning a new approach. The seven-button world. It rocks. She tries to throw a net over her thoughts to keep them from escaping, to think about the thing she has to think about, but they squirt through the mesh and go scooting off in every direction. This must be her time for faces, because faces start popping up from the dead leaves, from tree bark, from the blotchy patterns on her skin. Different faces. Devils, animals, a movie-star-looking guy with glossy hair. They all have the same wicked grin. It's beginning to bother her that she can't settle her mind. The calm she felt must have been a false calm, not the steady, solidifying calm that comes after the peak. Which means she hasn't peaked yet. She wonders if there's a remedy for peyote. Valium or something. Her jeans are soaked from the damp ground, her eyes itch, her legs are unaccountably sore. Maybe she should go inside. That could be rough. If she bumps into Jackson… Maybe she should eat first, maybe that would slow her head down. If he gives her one of his stern looks, she'll hurt herself laughing. And yet the thought of him, the basic concept of Jackson Bullard, alpha male fraud, husband, sobers her a hair. This is serious. For all its amateurish groping and bungling, her Nancy Drew-ish investigation of the paranormal may have terribly serious consequences, and, remembering the thing she needed to think about, the vortex, she turns toward the house, intending to give it the study it deserves.

The currents of the wind have multiplied and grown larger. They describe sweeping curves that transect the old house, passing through it, around and above it, seeming less currents than a single torsion, a translucent muscle shaped like a Moebius strip that is evolving into a knotted complexity, flowing faster and faster, increasing in size until its volume is three or four times that of the house. It tugs at Sanie, at something inside her, some crucial milligram of soul or spark trapped in the flesh, and its powerful pulse, though silent, is like the oscillations of those huge dynamos utilized in dams. She's so entranced by its power that, after realizing that this cannot possibly be the wind, she remains entranced for almost a half-hour, unmindful of its potentials, watching as it continues to expand, a great circularity that soon comes to fill all the air with a single disturbance. At length she achieves a distance from the event. There is nothing salubrious about this particular vortex, she decides, if that's what this monstrosity is. It harbors no tranquil spirit, it obscures no well of benign wisdom. It rages, broken from the rock, from the magma, from the planet's aether body, from some unguessable source, a random, aberrant discharge of energy, and if vortexes, vortices, or whatever attract spirits, or breed them, if an infant spirit is even now forming in this ravening womb, then by nature it's a collector, greedy and wholly self-absorbed; it acquires things, bright things that catch its eye and lend it coloration. In that, it reminds her of Jackson.

These thoughts seem like intuitions, ideas visited upon her, not the product of reason; but they make a kind of sense. Having a neutral value to begin with, the vortex must have derived its character from the Bullards. Had it been born on, say, a mountainside, a place frequented by antelope and birds and butterflies, or atop a Himalayan peak, it might have been a benign, salubrious vortex, but here in Culliver County, it's steeped in human corruption, in generational sin, and if it has come to incorporate a spirit, or if a spirit is awakening within it, then it is a Bullardian spirit, the great Demon Bullard taking shape in the spring of energy, bathing in its floods. The vortex is alarming, but she doesn't find it threatening. She doubts its capacity to harm her, unless she remains within its sphere of influence, and that's not something she will allow to happen.

Movement closer at hand, in the cornfield, distracts her. Wind shifting the stalks. She's been made wary by Janine's story about a herd of wild horses, but none materialize, no cattle or buffalo or Confederate troops. Just crows massing overhead, wheeling beneath the rain-sodden clouds, others flying up from the woods to join the flock, until hundreds of crows are circling the field in a black eddy. Are crows migratory? She supposes they are and that this massing presages a trip south to more temperate climes, to some crow paradise or vacationland where they will kick back on fences and play harmonicas, led in concert by the blind silver-eyed crow who plucks a strand of barbed wire to accompany his gravelly vocals, singing a dirge blues, "I killed a finch in Houston just to watch the feathers fly." A murder of crows, an extermination, a genocide of crows, gathering above her. She keeps an eye on them, anticipating an attack, but when they abruptly break off wheeling, moving in unison as might a school of fish, they aim straight for the house—they arrow down toward it and merge with the current of the vortex, becoming a black funnel that appears to be pouring itself through a kitchen window. The window isn't open, yet they pass through the panes without the least sign of breakage, the entire lunatic flock streaming inside and vanishing to the last straggler.

Sanie might not swear on a stack of Bibles that she saw

this, but she would wager a tidy sum on the proposition. She gets to her feet and stands rooted to the spot, waiting for the crows to reappear, but they do not, though the currents of the vortex wash gray, as if their passage has removed a trace of color from them or distilled their negative essence. It's too early to go in, but she has to risk it. She takes a step, teeters, and recognizes how stoned she is. After a tentative second step, a firmer third, she's walking with reasonable confidence over the half-frozen ground toward the house, which ripples and bulges, distortions that she's no longer convinced are hallucinatory. She can't see the currents of the vortex anymore, neither can she feel its pull, and that unnerves her. But it will be good inside, she tells herself. Warm. She, too, is half-frozen.

On reaching the rear of the house, she peeks in through a window. The kitchen contains its usual complement of table and chairs, sink, refrigerator. No broken crow bodies fluttering and bloody on the floor. No crows flapping against the walls or perched on the faucets and cupboards. They've flown to somewhere else or to nowhere at all. She steps through the door and, where nobody was a second before, there's Rayfield sitting at the table, poring over a newspaper. The sight jumps her heart rate, but she doesn't shrink from him. He's a younger version of himself, hair not yet completely gray; but, like the first time she saw him, he's naked. The heat is up so high, if he were alive he'd be comfortable. He turns the page. Folds it back, irons it flat with the heel of his before continuing to read. Exactly the way Jackson does it. The paper is the March 12, 1991, edition of the *Edenburg Courier*, an enterprise long since lapsed into bankruptcy.

The abstract pattern on the linoleum is floating up from the ochre tiles, and the whole room is busy with minute shiftings of a similar nature. Rayfield is the only stable form. The air's cooler close to him. Sanie eases through the door into the corridor, which looks no less unstable, the walls undulating, the wallpaper a pointillist confusion, but is unpopulated. The study door's open. Taking a chance, she peeks inside. Nary a Jackson in sight. She cracks the front door and discovers the SUV missing from its parking spot. He must have gone into town for copies—he'll be upset that she wasn't around to run the errand. She drops into his desk chair, grateful for the chance to relax amid this absence of Jackson. It occurs to her that she hasn't a clue what he's been doing in here. The words on the papers spread across the desktop hop about like fleas. She's not up to reading. In the shallow center drawer are pens, paper clips, thumb tacks, scissors, and so on. One side drawer is filled by a stack of skin magazines with slick, bright covers. The topmost displays two women who have just finished performing oral sex on a man, not depicted, and are licking copious amounts of fake sperm off each other's face. *Frosted Faces* reads the title in letters that resemble dripping ice cream.

"What the fuck," she says.

She examines the other magazines. *Bondage Sluts, Cum City Girls, Shaved Teenies,* and the like. Her personal favorite, *Cumlovers Anonymous,* features women (many of them portly) who are masked and blindfolded. Each is festooned with miniature Post-its, denoting pages—she assumes—with especially titillating pictures. From a second side drawer she unearths an entire series of a rag entitled *Oral Dungeon,* numbers I-XVI. So this is what he's been doing? Spanking the monkey to the tune of this crap? She can't believe it. They're Will's, probably. Or Rayfield's. Janine said he had some serious kinks. Yet maybe a taste for bondage runs in the family and Jackson's been repressing. A third drawer yields a stack of magazines devoted to horny housewives, girls next door, hitchhiking coeds, suburban moms. The fates of these innocents are not much different from those of their slutty counterparts. She leafs through one, pauses at a page to which a Post-it is affixed. She flips to another marked page, another, and another yet. She leafs through the entire magazine, a couple of magazines, and is led to the conclusion that all the women singled out for a Post-it in *Moms I'd Love To Fuck, No. 7* and *Cocksucker U* bear a strong resemblance to hers truly, Sanie Bullard. She's amused, she's sad, and then she's angry. As angry as the drug permits her to be. If these magazines belong to Jackson, as now she suspects they do… Her idea of hot fun does not involve being hogtied.

She slips the magazines back into the drawer. They're more information than she needs. There *is* a vortex. Whatever it's doing can't be good. That's the important stuff. Jackson's sexual predilections are no longer her concern. She grips the armrests and looks up, preparing to stand. Rayfield's bending over the desk, frowning, his liver-spotted face and glitter-pointed eyes inches away. Her heart jolts, she screams and shoves back the chair until it hits the bookcase. She swings her fist, trying to punch him and gives a yell, hoping to frighten him away. He winks out of existence. Alert to every flicker, every photic flaw in her vision, she steals toward the study door. The corridor is still empty. She stands listening to the house creaking like an old ship in a choppy sea, and then she pounds up the stairs, keeping her eyes low, not wanting to see what's waiting, ignoring the ghosts, the creatures of the vortex gathered to greet her with their frail subzero breath, and slams the bedroom door behind her, collapses on the bed. The dimness closes in, muffling her like a quilt, and she switches on a bedside lamp. Crummy yellow light, it hurts her eyes, but she leaves the lamp on, preferring it to the gloom.

Adrenaline has damped down her spaciness, but as she relaxes, feeling more secure, it returns. The walls play tricks, the wallpaper washes to the orange end of the yellow spectrum and its design of little red paddlewheelers begins to churn upstream, morphing into cowboys riding mechanical bulls. She has a memory of the mystic wood, of the silver flash she saw in the crotch of a hickory tree while passing through a gateway—she wishes now that she had gone in that direction, explored a silver dimension. The calm that she longed for earlier begins to settle over her. It's almost four o'clock, the digital radio on the night table tells her. That means she spent more than an hour in the study, because she recalls the kitchen clock said it was two-thirty when she came in from the cold. What a waste. More than an hour staring at cocks and pussies. The skin of the women felt warm in the photographs.

Jackson.

Her temper is tissue-thin as regards him. One moment she pities him, the next she thinks of him as a madman, and the next she's angry. When she comes down from her high, where will she be? Angry, she decides. Anger is the bedrock of their marriage. She realizes that now. Anger and betrayal. He betrays her by not being who he seemed, she betrays him by pretending to be who she is not and then acting like herself in secret. She doesn't want to think about the marriage, yet she can't stop herself. Who could have imagined that anger and betrayal would forge so powerful a bond. Stronger than love, than money, stronger than the matrimonial spell. It's an addiction, a sickness, a designer drug created by them, for them, and they couldn't quit using. But she has kicked it now. She'll make a last attempt at pulling Jackson out of Bullardonia, but it will be strictly pro forma. Want to go back to Chapel Hill? No? Okay. See ya.

She feels as though she's sinking deeper and deeper into the mattress, on the brink of being submerged, and has a sudden desire to be clean. With an effort, she staggers up and goes into the bathroom. A shower would be nice, but it can wait. She sheds her clothes and scrubs herself with a wash rag, clearing away a layer of scum. She examines her face. It's a disaster. The way she looks is partly due to the peyote and partly to the mirror, which is pitted, clouded, chipped, and warped... She, too, is pitted, clouded, chipped, and warped, albeit less permanently. She swabs at the mirror and succeeds in smearing soap across its surface. She takes a fresh rag, runs the tap over it, and scrubs harder. When she pauses to judge her work, the reflection staring back at her is Janine's.

She's become such an old hand at dealing with apparitions, she gives a start, but stops short of being shocked. She's horrified, mainly. The woman in the mirror is ten, fifteen years younger than Janine, her hair two shades redder, face agonized and mouth restrained by a ball gag. But it is definitely Janine. She lashes her head to and fro, her trophy breasts swaying, and bugs her blue eyes, trying to endure whatever is being done to her. And then she vanishes. Sanie retreats a step and turns to the bedroom. Sprawled on the bed, a leg hanging off the side, is a woman of late middle age wearing a blond wig, set slightly askew, and a poorly fitted Merry Widow—it's loose in the bodice, stretched tight over her pouchy belly, and cuts into the tops of her raddled thighs. The instant before the woman vanishes, Sanie spots red droplets on her lips and chin, a stippling of red on her chest. That tears it. Sanie can accept ghosts, but not the blood of Rayfield's victims. She bolts for the door, then remembers she's naked. She throws on a flannel shirt and searches for jeans, recalls that they're all in the wash. She puts on her cut-offs—she's in a panic and they fall to hand. It's only ten minutes walk to Snade's, she tells herself; she can withstand the cold for ten minutes. She shoulders her purse and, once again keeping her eyes low, goes out into the hall, out among the chill presences there, catching glimpses of their gaud and disarray as she tiptoes down the stairs, holding on to the banister.

The study door is closed.

Jackson's home.

He usually leaves the car keys beside the sink. She decides it's worth taking a look. She doesn't trust her eyes, can't tell if there's a seam of light beneath the kitchen door. She hesitates, then gives the door a tentative push. Jackson is sitting in Rayfield's chair, reading a paperback, and she thinks that, like Rayfield, he's naked, then realizes he's shirtless and wearing a pair of shorts. She's willing to bet that Rayfield also kept the house hot, and, if Jackson stays a few weeks longer, the shorts will be rendered passé.

"Hey," she says blithely, goes to the sink and scoops up the keys.

"Where you going?" he asks.

"Snade's. Want anything?"

"Snade's." He says it as he might the name of a great enemy. "I wondered why you got all dressed up."

I thought I'd go for a little spin, she thinks. Chapel Hill, New York, the world.

"All my jeans are in the wash," she says. "I'll only be outside for seconds, and I didn't think it would be a big deal. Okay?"

He shakes his head ruefully. "What in God's name is going on with you, Sanie?"

The harsh yellow light, as much as his question, rankles her, makes her imprudent. In that light the kitchen is the yellowest, ugliest room ever. Speckles and stains and discolorations, many of which aren't there to ordinary eyes. A hideous yellow cube full of hideous yellow objects.

"What's going on with me? I'm going to Snade's," she says. "I was thinking maybe I'd get a couple of beers, but then I thought… Wait for it! This is big. Then I thought… chips. What do you think? It's a tough decision and I need a second opinion. Chips? Or pretzels?"

"Sanie." Another head-shake. How he's suffered. The intemperate behavior he's been forced to overlook.

She can't stop, the peyote's got her all brave and snippy. "I figure it'd be best to make an on-the-spot decision. An informed judgement. Give the bags a squeeze. Check the expiration dates."

"Sanie." He turns to her. His face is a mess. It looks as if he's an actor half-done putting on his Quasimodo make-up. "The way you're acting… I can't get a handle on you."

She mocks his southern accent by thickening her own. "I just can't get a handle on you, neither."

A sigh. "I wish you could see me, Sanie."

His inflection, redolent of paternal regret and tenderness, chills her.

"I wish you'd prune back your craziness a little," he says. "I wish you'd purge yourself of all the frantic garbage that gets in the way of your thinking straight, and take a serious look at me. You have to look deep, look close. You used to be able to look right into my soul, but nowadays you don't even give me a glance."

The chill spreads throughout her body, weakening her knees. Because it was so soft, she thinks, hardly more than a whisper, the ghost voice never conveyed the undertone of menace that floors Jackson's voice.

"One glimpse is all you'll need to remind you of who I am," he says. "Why'nt you take a look?"

She starts for the door, but he flings out an arm, blocking her path, and she backs against the sink.

"You're afraid of me?" His laugh rides a little high and cracks. "Don't be afraid, Sanie. There's nothing to be afraid of."

"I'm not afraid." She irons out a quaver in her voice. "I'm thirsty."

She walks around the opposite side of the table to avoid his arm, and he stands.

"If only you could see me, Sanie, I know you'd understand."

Despite the broken record aspect of his words, his creepy tone of voice, anger shows in his face. At last. A genuine emotion. He positions himself in such a way that he can block her, whichever route she chooses. The rear door… She thinks she can make it. He sometimes locks the screen door, but she's so terrified, she's ready to bust through it. She recognizes how foolish she's been to be afraid of him all these years, yet never believe he would hurt her.

"Let me get my beer," she says. "We can talk after."

"Why won't you look at me, Sanie?"

"I am looking, okay?" She inches toward the door; she'll sprint into the woods, where he'll never find her. "What are you doing, Jackson? I love you."

That flusters him, interrupts the rhythms of his madness. His mask, his inch-deep pose of masculine gentleness and fond regard, shatters and something is revealed beneath that terrifies her even more; and yet it seems inadequate to the moment, dismasted by her declaration of love. She thinks she should repeat it. Maybe that will sedate him. But she's so frightened and the rear door is so close… She springs for it and wrenches it open, punches out the screen with her elbow while fumbling with the catch. He hauls her back, slings her against the sink, and she goes down onto the floor. She crawls behind the table, scrambles to her feet. For the space of four or five seconds, they watch one another across the table, breathing heavily, and she senses some heretofore unstated principle hardening between them, a fundamental enmity exposed. She darts toward the inner door and he drags her back a second time, tries to hit her with his fist, misses… but his forearm slams into her shoulder and drives her sideways. Her head smashes the glass front of a cupboard. She stumbles away, glass in her hair, dazed and blinded by blood, clawing at his face, and feels a tremendous blow on her temple.

White light splinters behind her eyes. She doesn't lose consciousness, but she can't tell where she is. Floating, it seems. Stretched out and floating. Like a woman levitated by a magician. Gradually she becomes aware that she's lying on the floor. Jackson kneels beside her, saying things she can't understand due to the ringing in her ears. She doesn't have to hear them; she's heard them whispered ever since she arrived. He hooks his arms beneath her armpits, lifts her, clamps a hand behind her back for support, as if they're about to whirl out on a dance floor. She's so dizzy, she doesn't care what's going on. She's sick to her stomach, too, and, when he lifts her again, balancing her on his shoulder, using her legs to bump open the kitchen door, she thinks she might throw up; but she passes out instead.

The world fades in again, illumined by a less harsh yellow light. Her temple throbs and a male voice is droning on and on, making the throbbing worse. Blearily, she identifies the bedroom by a water stain on the ceiling. Her face is damp—someone has wiped the blood from her eyes. She can't pull her thoughts together. Thrashing about, she discovers that she's secured, wrist and ankle, to the bedposts. She screams, tries to yank a wrist free, and Jackson moves into her field of vision. He's removed his shorts and is half-erect. He talks to her in that namby-pamby voice, that fake, fatherly tone. She screams again as he climbs onto the bed and positions himself between her thighs. "No… don't!" she says tearfully. His cock butts her inner thigh. Revulsion sparks a panic. Her mind seems to short out and, once awareness returns, she finds that his erection has wilted. His battered face is suspended above her, taut with rage and frustration. Something takes shape in the air behind him, waxing from a smudge of color into a disembodied presence—withered neck, a shawl of gray hair, piece of chin, an eye. A decaying grin centers these relics and she has the idea that Rayfield is leaning over Jackson's shoulder, urging him to complete the violation, adding the force of his dementia to his son's. Then, beside her, the Merry Widow pops into view. The old woman struggles to breathe, coughing up droplets of blood. Her throat is bruised and oddly indented. Powder caked on her sunken cheeks, her wig tipped over one eye as though in drunken abandon. Giving in to fright, Sanie bucks her hips wildly, hoping to unseat Jackson, and he begins to beat her. It's a dispassionate beating. Workmanlike. With his features lumped and empurpled, he's a mutant from a low-budget sci-fi movie. A mutant pounding nails. He pins her by the neck and throws the punches one at a time, methodically. They land on her hips, ribs, and stomach, robbing her of breath, of voice. It feels as if he's killing her, and she wants to scream, but she's reduced to staring dumbly at him, scratchy noises in her throat generated by each impact. Saliva hangs a thick string from his parted lips and flaps about when he hits her. He emits a grunt with every blow, very like the grunts he makes when he comes. Shadows pass across his face, or it might be they're passing across the surface of her eyes. Pain drives her into hiding.

When she regains her senses, she wishes she hadn't. Her body aches all over and she has a wicked spike of pain beneath her left breast. Voices in the hall. Through the half-open door, she spots Jackson, naked. Will in his robe. And Frank Dean. Wearing coveralls. She tries to call out, but still can't find her voice. He's carrying a lug wrench. Holding it up beside his head and staring balefully at someone. He moves forward, vanishes, and Louise comes into frame. They're all ghosts, Sanie thinks. Will, Jackson, Louise, herself, Frank Dean. Whether actually there or not, they're ghosts. Creatures of the vortex. Controlled by that mighty engine, an ancient ghost wafts by, two-thirds of a fat dowager with a crepey throat, wearing shreds of a ball gown. She hovers beside the latest generation of Bullards, as though interested in their problem, preparing to offer advice.

Jackson notices Sanie watching and slams the door. The muffled voices lull her and she loses track of things. She wakes after an indefinite time and can't hear them talking anymore. Her head feels huge, balloonlike, with a pulse in her temple rapid as a bird's, yet her mental clarity is better than it has been. She looks at her right wrist. The knot's a relatively simple one. She pushes herself up, bracing against the headboard, and gasps with the pain that lances her left side. She stretches her neck, trying to reach the knot with her teeth. So close. Frustrated tears start from her eyes, but she keeps at it. On her fifth try, she snags the knot and bites down and begins worrying at it. The velvet tie around one ankle comes loose from the bedpost and that makes things easier; but she has to enlist all her determination and her strength to untie her other ankle. She'd like to collapse, but doubts she'll survive if she does. Favoring her left side, she limps to the closet and takes down a dress with buttons in front. She shrugs into it, ever so slowly, buttons a few of the buttons. Puts on a coat the same way. Then she remembers her purse, her cell phone. She empties the purse on top of the bureau. Jackson's taken the phone. Wobbly, she rests her head against the bureau. It's obvious that she can expect no assistance from Will or Louise. Will must have alerted Jackson to her intentions—that must have been what he meant when he said, "I expect we should help him." But then she realizes that if he did tell Jackson, he did so not because of any reason she might think of—it's something ridiculous. Some elliptical, daffy logic that would make sense only to Will and the rest of Bullard Nation.

In the depths of the closet, against the back wall, there's a collection of walking sticks. She paws around inside it, hanging onto the door, and clutches at them, gathers three. Soft white pine with knobbly grips, whittled and sanded smooth by Rayfield. Under any other circumstance, she would be loathe to touch them. She chooses one to lean on, another to use as a weapon, and hobbles toward the door, every step, every muscular action, a new adventure in pain. When she started out, she thinks, it was just about a ten-minute walk to Snade's; now it's going to take forever.

NINETEEN

Descending the stairs one at a time, Sanie's afraid of being caught, but she is not afraid of what will happen if she's caught. Jackson has hurt her, she believes, as badly as she can be hurt short of killing her. Her ears are ringing, the pain in her side is worsening, her jaw is swollen and aching, her vision is blurred, and she's scarcely able to walk—symptoms that do not augur well. She no longer thinks she's risking much by seeking to escape, and she wishes that she had arrived at this conclusion sooner.

She lowers her right leg onto a step and braces against the banister, then eases the left side of her body down, careful not to plant her foot too heavily, or else her hip will send a shriek of pain up into her spine; and when she reacts to that, something—a rib, probably—stabs her deep. She's almost at the bottom of the stairs when she hears voices issuing from the study, through the partly open door. Four voices, all speaking at once, the most assertive belonging to Jackson, the once and future Bullard, the newest Bullard of Bullard Hall. Sanie can tell they're arguing, but she doesn't listen. She concentrates on her cautious movement, on the next step, and the next.

Miraculously, she makes it past the study without being seen. A quick glance into the room reveals Will's back blocking all of the potential sightlines. It's gone dark outside. Once down the road a piece, she can go into the fields and hide. She reaches the bottom of the stairs and minimizes the creaking of the front door. On the porch, she rests her head on a support post, gathering herself. It's only three steps to the ground, but there's no banister to grab onto and she's worried that she will fall. The wood is cool on her brow, seeming to transmit solidity, strengthening her. She thinks ahead to Snade's and her buddy Gar. She pictures his solicitude, feels the warmth of the store, and imagines he'll offer a restorative drink of some pigsty bourbon, for which she'll be unendingly grateful. And a telephone. She'll be all over that phone. The shit is going to hit the fan at Bullard Hall. Assault, unlawful restraint, drug possession, rape. She hopes Jackson likes jumpsuits. He's going to be wearing a nice bright orange one the next few years.

"Sanie."

Galvanized by fear, and then driven by a fury like none she's felt before, she drops one of the sticks and swings the business end of the other two-handed toward the sound of Jackson's voice, striking him on the hinge of his jaw. Her momentum causes her to totter off-balance and she fetches up against the door frame, crying out from a knifing agony under her ribs. Jackson is spun away from her, clutching his jaw and cursing. Fueled by a murderous conviction, Sanie rights herself, ignores the pain, and, as he turns toward her, swings the stick again, bringing it down onto the crown of his head. His knees give way and he crumples, slumping onto his side, moaning. Will, Allie, and Louise stand in the hallway behind him, displaying stupefaction.

"Stay back!" Sanie retreats toward the porch steps, shuffling her feet in baby steps, holding the stick out to menace them. She hooks an arm around a post and heels open the screen door. Will lurches forward and she shouts at him, not threats, not curses, but meaningless noises such as you might yell when driving a dog away from a garbage can. He's confused by her rage, which is a good thing, because she has to lower herself to one knee and half-crawl, backing down the steps. She hobbles to the gate, checking over her shoulder to see if they're in pursuit. Thrown into silhouette by the light spilling from the doorway, it appears they're pawing at Jackson, clumsy as bears playing with a fresh kill.

Out on the road, charged with the glee she feels at having coldcocked him, she picks up the pace and seems to glide over the bumpy track, nearly pain-free. Son-of-a-bitch, she says to herself. Pissant freak. And what is the deal with Allie? An honorary Bullard? Another victim-in-waiting? Will and Louise, now them she can understand, blood being thicker than water and all. Judging by her brief conversation with Louise, it's possible to conclude that Rayfield abused her. Which would account for her erratic loyalty. When the cops come, they'll see she's not competent and lock her away. That's sad, if true. But Sanie can't afford to care.

She approaches the curve and the pain begins to take hold again. She's cold, she's losing coordination. She grows increasingly giddy and disoriented, meandering from one side of the road to the other. The potholes are killing her. She's into the curve, right in the blind spot where Frank Dean almost ran her down, when she admits to herself that she won't make it to Snade's. Not without a rest. She locates the ditch she fell into when Frank Dean nearly ran her over and, laboriously, with rickety grace, she lays herself down and arranges leaves and twigs over her body as best she can. It's cold and the ground is hard, but the hum of traffic from the state road and the smell of the damp earth and moldering leaves weave a blanket that seems to muffle her discomfort. She drifts in and out. Before long, a car rolls slowly past from the direction of the house. She watches the taillights fade. The SUV. A minute or two later, it returns, going at high speed. She can't make out who's driving. Things are hopping at Bullard Hall.

She brushes leaves from her face so she can see more clearly, not that there's a lot to see. Big ugly shapes writhe in the clouds, like snakes in pregnant black bellies. She's still tripping. Solitude closes in on her and a tear leaks out. She wishes someone would help her, that she had someone she could count on.

Nope, she tells herself. Not going there.

Tonight self-pity is against the rules.

Which rules are those?

Survival.

Oh, that.

A friend, though. That would be good. A friend you could count on.

There ain't no such animal.

Fuck cynical! Just because you're cynical doesn't make you right.

You've had your chances. With Brittany, Howard, Brenda Havers back in Carboro, and maybe Frank Dean. Plenty of others, too. You always held back, you always chose the wrong people.

Maybe next time.

Is that fatalism talking? No fatalism allowed, either. You're going to be fine. It's a short haul to Snade's.

She remembers going to the store... What was it? The fourth time she went in? Before people were used to her, anyway. Before she was used to them. A teenage boy followed her along the aisles, gawking, and one of the old farts in front, an extremely old fart wearing bib overalls and a baseball cap announcing his allegiance to the Myrtle Beach Pelicans, scolded him, saying, "Ain't you never seen a pretty gal, son? Whyn't you learn to be more discrete? That way you might get you one." When she came to the counter to pay for her Diet Pepsi, he grinned at her and then made a grab for his heart, feigning an attack... A twinge of pain interrupts the memory. She should get going, she thinks. The SUV might make another pass, but she figures it's more likely, more Bullardesque, that they'll become distracted and neglect the situation. They'll spend an hour debating what to do and then both get to screwing Allie while Louise looks on.

She starts walking again.

Fifteen minutes and fifty yards into the second leg of her journey, she's breathing shallowly to avoid aggravating her side. Her thoughts scatter like feathers in a wind. She has to pause on occasion to reassure herself that she hasn't gotten turned around and is not heading back toward the Bullard house. Under her breath, she sings Tom Petty, Tina, Lucinda Williams, the two Elvises. She sticks to mid-tempo stuff, so she doesn't risk catching Dance Fever.

Heh, heh.

Thank you, thank you very much,

What Becomes Of The Broken-Hearted is they wind up walking with a stick at an eighth of a mile an hour down a dirt road that might just be the Highway To Hell...

Not funny.

If you can't please yourself, who can you please?

She doesn't have the answer.

Another fifty yards and she'll see how she feels.

It takes her more than fifteen minutes to travel that fifty yards, but she thinks she's found a rhythm. She gets along by plotting a course. Pothole ahead. Jog to the right. Is that a rut? Yes. Better angle left. Fixating on the mechanical process of walking helps her to ignore her physical problems. Occasionally a bright pain causes her to catch her breath, but she manages it. She managed the stairs, after all. Horizontal's a lot easier than up or down. But it's a thin confidence. She understands that. Behind it, exhaustion is pressing in on her.

She spots what she supposes to be a pothole and, forgetting where she is in the road, angles her path to the left. It's a bad mistake. She's walking a stretch of road that is elevated a couple of feet above the fields it traverses, and, when she plants her weak leg, her foot hits on the downslope and throws her off-balance. She tries to catch herself and goes reeling across the field, each ungainly step doing damage to her rib and hip, and falls heavily, twisting at the last second to take the impact on her right side. Pain consumes her. She bridges up from the mucky ground, every muscle tensed, but she can't reduce the pain to a controllable level. It's like she's burning, her nerves all firing at once, yielding a white light into which she dissolves.

On waking, she's cold, but there's nothing she can do about it. Her side throbs and she doesn't believe she can move. Moving's not on her current Ten Things I Do Best list, at any rate. She discovers she can use her arms without causing herself much pain and levers herself up so that her head is resting against a stump, affording her a view of, basically, very little. Darkness flocked by pinpricks of light. She's lying in the open, visible from the road, but there's nothing she can do about that, either. Her body seems to have achieved a precarious inner equilibrium and she's afraid to disturb it.

Her legs are really cold.

Deal with it.

When the tough get going, the weird turn pro.

Got milk.

Militant Bitch!

No! Fuck you!

I'm in the mood for (g)love.

God looks like Bea Arthur.

…pretty, sexy, chaste, and reckless, taller than the T in Texas…

If you buy me a beer, I'll let you… finish my homework.

This recitation of T-shirts worn during her all-too-brief wild-child phase ends when she reaches: If you love something, let it go… then hunt it down and kill it.

It's as if every channel in her brain leads to Jackson.

That's going to change, she swears. She'll scrub him off her and never look back. She tries to think warm thoughts, pictures herself in the Caribbean somewhere, sunbathing in her red bikini, but that doesn't do it for her.

What would Jesus do?

Perform a magic act. Change dead grass into Maker's Mark. Give himself up to the Roman soldiers.

Scratch Jesus.

How about Buddha?

Buddha wouldn't have this problem.

The SUV rolls by again and Sanie tries to shrink, to merge with the ground. Amazingly, they don't see her. She must be far enough off the road that she's not easy to see, or else they're wearing special Bullard Vision goggles. Maybe it's just too dark. Once the SUV has gone, she collects sticks, leaves, grass, and covers herself as she did in the ditch. She can't reach her lower legs, so they're left bare. She's freezing, but she would rather be here than tied to Jackson's bed. She recalls how it felt to hit him, the ferocity of the swing, the conviction and accuracy of the blows. Instinct. If she had acted on instinct years ago… but she didn't. There's no point in imagining what might have been. She's spent too much time playing that game as it is. She's weary, overtaxed, and she doesn't attempt to resist when a black wave of sleep, or something like sleep, carries her under.

She wakes and discovers that the sky has washed clear of clouds, gone a deep electric blue. Stars are shining and the moon, a fat silver crescent like a toy canoe, is low in the southern sky. Her covering of grass and twigs begins to itch and she brushes most of it off. The itching subsides, but the bad news is, the exertion wears her out. There's not going to be any tap-dancing down to Snade's after a nap. The good news, she's not as cold as she was. At least she thinks it's good news.

A piece of a weed, a couple inches of stem and one shriveled brown floret, is stuck to the side of her hand. Three flowers the size of seed pearls are crammed together, clutched by a vegetable talon, looking like a single bloom until she brings it close. A complex, worthless beauty, its cunning design all for naught. She wipes it off on her coat.

It's going to be okay, she tells herself.

She hangs with the moon, floating above the line of hickory and elms at one end of the field. There aren't enough stars to make the usual constellations, so she arranges those available into a sky-spanning one, a Picasso construction. She can't think of a name for it.

The Death Of Don Quixote. Don Quixote Tells A Joke In The Afterlife Cafe. Don Quixote's Joke Wedded To A Corporate Business Graph.

It's more Paul Klee than a Picasso, she decides.

What will Mama say?

Look sad, stroke Sanie's hair, and say, "I should have known."

Brittany... Well, Sanie's taking her off speed dial. Howard will simply gape.

She drowses and wakes with a start, heart pounding, certain that a car is coming. But no car appears. It might have been an animal noise that disturbed her. A fox or a possum sniffing her toes. The sky's losing its deep blue, shading to gray in the east. She watches the gray turn pink, conch-shell pink, then rosy pink. They'll be coming soon. The Bullards. Straight from their appearance at The Psycho Lounge.

Again, not funny.

Yet that's who she married into—the bunch from *The Hills Have Eyes*, hillbilly mutants with a touch of aristocratic polish.

Overhead, a cloud is forming, a thready structure spinning itself out of nothing, like a strand of silk woven by an invisible spider. Some crucial portion of her being, part of her mind, her soul, strains toward the cloud, balloons like a sail filling with wind, bearing her outward on a wave of intense yearning, neither sad nor exultant, an emotion free of imperfection, the desire to be everywhere, to touch everything. She rides it up and up, and then snaps back into the body, steadying now. Solid again. The idea that she might have been letting go, that letting go was an option, frightens her. She tries to find something to hook onto, to find an anchor. The moon, bone pale, is almost down, riding in the crown of a leafless elm, as if the silver canoe got caught in it and all that's left of it is this skeletal memento mori. Her eyes lock onto it for the longest time.

Wasn't there a nursery rhyme about a silver boat caught in a tree? If not, there should be. Little Sanie Bullard went away to sea, and her pretty silver boat got caught up in a tree, a family tree, on the far side of Tralee, beyond the Zuider Zee, in a land of mystery...

South Carolina, Land of Mystery.

Down every dirt road, a monster.

The cadence of that thought reminds her of a Bryan Ferry song, "In Every Dream Home a Heartache," and she tries to remember the lyrics.

Like when you rub away condensation from a patch of windshield and see an unexpected shadow standing by the hood of your car, she suddenly sees what's ahead. She can't see clearly—its outlines and dimensions are indistinct—but she understands, she knows, she can feel the knowledge growing inside her, cold and keen, an ice crystal evolving, its frozen structures spreading all through her blood, and it hurts the way loneliness hurts, it hollows her chest and drops a stone into the hollow and that stone weighs more than her life ever did. Her life was merely the splash the stone made in falling. She seizes up, like a mouse confronting a snake, blinking its black eyes, not sure which way to run. She can't even say it to herself, she can't speak its name. Saying would make it so, and that's her sole remaining refuge now, in stillness and a childlike magic.

A car engine downshifting, coming from the direction of the house, breaks the spell, and Sanie averts her eyes, not wanting to see Jackson, twice-battered now, resembling a lumped, enraged mutant. The first time she saw him, he was beautiful. She hears brakes applied, a door opening.

"Sanie!"

Her vision is still blurred, all soft focus like a Hollywood representation of a dream, but dimmer and flickering at the edges. Frank Dean kneels beside her. When he goes to cradle her head, pain saws though her insides and she cries out.

"Don't!" she says. "Don't touch me!"

He tugs at her dress. It's all bunched up around her hips. Everything's showing and she's dreadfully embarrassed, she wishes he wasn't seeing her like this, and she wants to explain. He drapes his jacket over her legs, asking who hurt her, then digs in his trouser pocket. "Shit!" he says. He leans close and says, "I left my cell at the shop. I'm going to get help."

"Stay," she says, fumbling for his hand.

"You need a doctor. I'm…"

"Please. Jackson's coming."

"Did he do this?"

Warmth and wetness between her thighs. She's peed herself.

"I'm sorry," she says, and then doesn't know what she meant, she has so much to be sorry about.

The light is graying overhead. She's comforted by Frank Dean's smell of tobacco and strong soap. It seems that several minutes pass before he speaks.

"Sanie," he says. "I've got to get you some help."

Another car coming from the same direction. The SUV pulls up behind Frank Dean's van. It sits, idling. No one climbs out. The driver shifts into reverse and backs toward the house, weaving, nearly running off the road is his haste to be gone.

Sanie tries to speak and Frank Dean says, "What?"

She wants to say, What a dumbass Jackson is! He should be hightailing it, not returning to the house. She wants to tell Frank Dean about the Bullards, what astonishing fuck-ups they are, but it would take too long.

"I know where I can use the phone," says Frank Dean with quiet resolve. "Don't you worry about Jackson."

She closes her eyes. There are no stars in her darkness, only silvery crackles, thoughts lighting the midnight of a brain. Important thoughts, like lines in a notebook she doesn't want to forget. Like the ant and the chain-link fence. Lines that stood for something and now she can't remember what.

"Sanie?"

She wants to answer, but she's slipping away again, being pulled toward something, an irresistible pull... She resists it, anyway, clinging to Frank Dean's smell, to the memory of an older smell, Vicks Vap-o-Rub, to the solid earth (she can hardly tell it's spinning), to the image of palm nut in an African hand, a photograph of a tiger, somebody reverently touching her face...

"Hey, Sanie!"

...and then she can resist no longer, she releases into the pull, lets the current take her wherever it's bound, into its great curving circuit...

"Sanie? Sanie?"

She wonders why she isn't more afraid.

EPILOG

...Sanie... Sanie...

Mostly Sanie's not there, and when she is there, she doesn't know where there is. A house with many chambers, old and ill-kept. It's familiar, but that's all she knows, except that she doesn't like it much. She has the idea she's being cared for, but she can't recall by whom, and that she's recovering from an injury, though she's uncertain as to its nature. She thinks they're giving her drugs that impair the memory, or it could be her memory is impaired and they're medicating her to restore it. She has the same scraped, pared-down feeling that she had on... some drug or another, she can't recall. Everything seems vague and imponderable. Even common household objects pose mysteries that she must plumb.

She's lonely, yet she's never alone. She has the impression that a number of people are close by. She apprehends them, somehow, but she can't see them, and she suspects they're watching her, analyzing her behavior. She doesn't enjoy being watched, even when it's for her own good, but she supposes it's necessary. The only person she does see is the man who calls to her incessantly and follows her about. He seems familiar, too, but she can't pin down where they met. He's annoying. He calls and calls, and when he finds her in the kitchen (as he generally does), he loses interest—it's as if all he wants is to make certain of her presence—and wanders off. She doesn't like him much, either. She keeps meaning to speak to him, to tell him that she doesn't appreciate him hawking her, but when they're together, she's intimidated, she refuses to look at him, she doesn't want to make things worse.

...Sanie...

She feels disappointed when she's there. And not just a little bit. Horribly, miserably disappointed. What she's disappointed about is not so clear. It's like a word on the tip of her tongue, one she's certain she'll remember soon, but that she always forgets to remember. And maybe that's a blessing, she thinks. She has the sense that it's something she wanted to forget. So she feels disappointed... and pulled. Drawn toward the kitchen. The man's nagging voice nudges her that way, but it's more as if she's being pulled by a force that she can't fathom, a current that carries her along. Once she's better, she's confident she'll understand why she's disappointed and why she has to visit the kitchen. Actually, her time in the kitchen is the one thing she enjoys about being there. After the man has gone back to wherever he goes, that is. She sits at the table and stares at the Cumberland Farm Supplies calendar on the refrigerator. It's open to the November page. In the picture a woman stands on the porch, holding a mixing bowl and scanning a barren field, as if she is expecting someone or searching for signs of life. The field is huge, a thousand furrows, a dirt front yard that stretches away to a dark line in the distance. Trees, one would imagine, but it could be a vast army or a wall. The woman is stirring the bowl as she looks out across the field and, though it's a cheerless image, Sanie thinks it's intended as a reminder of Thanksgiving, that the woman is a farm wife putting the finishing touches on her meal, concerned about her family, hoping the turkey won't dry out by the time they return.

What Sanie likes above all things when she's there is interpreting the picture various ways. Making up stories about the woman. She's more vital, more alive, when she's so engaged. Post-apocalyptic farm wife; widowed farm wife; a farm wife who murders her family with the poisoned batter she's mixing in the bowl; she runs through the most obvious, pulpiest interpretations and then creates a storyline about a farm wife who's married to a man she doesn't love, who doesn't want to be a farm wife, but can't figure out how to be anything else. Her dreams and hopes seem unattainable, yet she believes she would attain them if she could bring herself to drive down the road that cuts across the field. The road isn't in the picture, but Sanie knows it's there, otherwise no one could reach the house… then maybe that's the problem. Maybe the dark line in the distance is, in fact, a wall, an impenetrable wall the farm wife helped to build, and now she can't leave unless she discovers the secret that will penetrate it, a special key, a piece of magic that will destroy the wall, cause it to dissolve into mist and let the world flood in. That's what the farm wife wants. She wants to divorce her husband and marry the world, she wants the world to come inside her, to flow through and around her, she wants to breathe in its currents. Sanie's disappointed that she can't get beyond this point in the story. She'd hate to believe it's the end, that the farm wife is trapped. She thinks if she could write it down, if she had a pen, she could write her way out of this corner and arrive at a proper ending. But she has no pen. She assumes pens are not allowed and she chafes at this regulation. She determines to say something to the man about it when next he appears, although she doubts he'll be able to do anything.

Lacking a pen, she wishes she could turn the page on the calendar. December might offer a picture less bleak than November's and more open to interpretation. But she senses that if she attempts to turn the page, to break her routine the least bit, she will be sent back upstairs. This rule, she's certain, is a strict rule, one that may not and, possibly, cannot be broken. It may be that it's for her own good. December's picture might not be to her liking. And so she sits, puzzling over the image of the farm wife and the barren field. She thinks that it may be a test. If she can create a satisfactory ending to the farm wife's story, she will be released, pronounced well and fit to travel. She chips away at the task, fitting an ending to the story and tossing it aside, fitting and tossing aside, fitting and tossing. They don't seem organic outgrowths of the plot, too hastily carpentered, absurdly Pollyanna-ish, or else they involve ridiculous Deus ex Machinas, but she keeps at it despite the eternally lowering overcast of her mood, a hint of nervousness creeping into her efforts, worry eroding her ability to reason, hoping that she can finish before she's whisked back upstairs and the man goes to calling her name and it starts all over again. It's so awful there. The people she can't see are pressing in on her, peering over her shoulder, and the man won't ever let her be. She'd give anything for a pen. And a notebook. With a notebook, she might be able to work on the story when she's away from the kitchen. She knows she has to work fast, she knows it can all be taken away from her at any moment. One second she's there, and then she's not.